The Story of Ma

ISBN: 9798520223924

Unless otherwise indicated, all scripture quotations are from the King James Version, KJV, of the Bible.

Unless otherwise indicated, all Quran quotations are from the ClearQuran (clearquran.com).

Cover by Fahri Pelit (Instagram #fahripelit).

Illustrations by Fahri Pelit and Inge Koltes.

First Edition.

Dedicated to refugees throughout this world.
May they find peace of mind, safety, security,
new life, acceptance, and supply of their
needs in the lands to which they have fled.

The Truth can be denied by the majority for a certain amount of time, or by some people forever, but it can never be hidden from everyone forever. This is the lesson of History, which has inexorably revealed the great crimes of the past and those who perpetrated them.

— Carlo M. Vigano

Contents

Acknowledgements

Thank you Mahmoud for your insights into Iraqi history and sharing your knowledge about Rawa, Ramadi, and Baghdad. Thanks for contributing from your own personal experiences at Ramadi University and later in India, and then returning home to lead a group of Iraqi refugees across ISIS held territory in Syria and into Turkey. Most of all, thanks for the years you have worked tirelessly helping Afghani, Iraqi, and Syrian refugees in Turkey. You are an inspiration to many.

Thank you Deborah Rays for your valuable contributions to the story.

Special thanks to editors Rose, Croil, Lona, Luz, Rey and Joyce, not just for your editing, but also for your valuable input.

Thanks to my friends, the team at Safe Haven for Refugees and my wonderful siblings who have helped launched this book! Love to my kids and grandkids. May all your dreams for a better world come true!

Foreword

The backdrop for *The Story of Mahmoud* is based on documented historical events. Mahmoud is a real person, and we used some parts of his life in this book. But this book is a composite of the true experiences of numerous people who were affected by the same events in Iraq, or by the Syrian Civil War. These are all blended into the life of the main character, Mahmoud.

This is the uncensored story of people growing up and living through terrible times, of people who lose livelihoods and family members during those times, and who firmly believe that these tragic losses were for no good reason or purpose, that a peaceful alternative to war could have been found. It is their hope, and ours, that this story will give us the strength and motivation to work for peaceful solutions to conflict.

There is a Documentation appendix at the end of the book which provides additional facts and information about the actual events mentioned in the story.

Introduction

The time was late summer 2014. I was visiting Romania to escape the hot and humid weather in southern Turkey where our charity was running an education center for the deaf. I also was assisting some small programs for Syrian refugees who had been moving into our city.

After hiking the beautiful Carpathian Mountains, I headed back to Bucharest for a few days before flying back to Istanbul. I checked into a hostel in downtown Bucharest operated by a Christian charity. The price was affordable and the people were friendly.

When the staff at the little hostel found out that I lived and worked in Turkey, I was soon assaulted by a million and one questions about what it is like to live in Turkey amongst Muslims, many of whom they regarded as terrorists. They had many questions about the Syrians, asking if it was dangerous where I worked. Some were of the opinion that most Syrian young men were either Al Qaeda, Nusra, Hezbollah, or Daesh, the Arabic acronym for ISIS.

I fielded their questions patiently explaining my experience with the warm and friendly young people of Syria and Turkey whom I work with. I was thus invited to speak at their youth get-together the following day.

The next day, I presented a PowerPoint of our work to the Romanian youth, showing the wonderful, smiling Turkish volunteers serving the disadvantaged in a wide variety of projects. But somehow they kept coming back to the mantra "Muslims are terrorists."

An inspiration came to me to tell them a story, as stories can sometimes get a point across much better than simple explanations. The following is the story of Mahmoud, though in much greater detail than the story I told that warm evening in Bucharest.

The tale is based on painfully true events that occurred in Iraq over the last forty years. It documents a life filled with countless sorrows and hardships, set against the backdrop of continual war, civil unrest, and foreign occupation. It is a must-read for anyone who wants to experience firsthand what it is like to grow up under the effects of war, being a victim of the reckless and ill-planned foreign policies of other countries.

My hope is that this story, told in Mahmoud's own words, will help you see the world from the perspective of a child growing up in the Middle East and that it will answer a question that begs to be asked: "Who is the terrorist?"

> Write History now, before it is rewritten, erased or buried!
>
> — Jon Rose

1

Iraq—The Cradle of Civilization

So Begins Mahmoud's Story . . .

My family and the main characters:

Father—Died in the Iran-Iraq War, 1988.
Mother—The greatest cook, she kept us together.
Mohammed—Born 1973; the eldest sibling.
Abdullah—Born 1978; the brother I was closest to.
Linda—Born 1980; my sister who loved to spoil me.
Rana—Born 1982; my sister, we would talk for hours.
Mahmoud—Born November, 1984; that's me!
Mariam—Born 1988; my little sister, our joy.
Grandfather—The Wise Counsellor.
Cousin Mustafa—The Musician.

"In the name of God, the infinitely Compassionate and the most Merciful"[1] are the first words I remember learning after learning the names of my immediate family. My grandfather would put me on his knees and teach me the 99 names of God, telling me how each name is an attribute

---

[1] الرحيمالرحمان الله بسم Bismillah ar-Rahman ar-Raheem

of our merciful Creator. The names "ar-Rahman" and "ar-Raheem" are especially important as they mean God is the Most Merciful and the Most Compassionate, and so we must live like Him, showing mercy and compassion.

Grandfather would tell me how God is the Lord of the Worlds. I loved listening to Grandfather explain to me the opening words of the Fatiha, which is the main prayer of the Koran. When he would talk about the Mercy, Compassion and Generosity of God, his words would bring me to another world, a land of light, where everything was beautiful, where there was no sorrow or pain. His words could paint such a picture in my mind. He had such a serenity about him, and he became like a father to me as my dad was off at war on the Iran/Iraq front line and away most of the time.

We lived in Rawa, a beautiful ancient town on the

Euphrates River. When Grandfather would talk of the beauties of Cennet and Paradise, I could not imagine anything more beautiful than Rawa. I spent the earliest years of my life in Rawa.

To help you understand Rawa, I need to digress and tell

you the fascinating history of Iraq, a country full of incredible antiquity and culture. Known as the Cradle of Civilization, the location of mankind's first urban centers, its history can be traced back for 10,000 years.

During ancient times, the lands that now constitute Iraq were known as Mesopotamia, which means "The Land Between the Rivers," a region whose extensive alluvial plains gave rise to some of the world's earliest great civilizations, including those of Sumer, Akkad, Babylon, and Assyria. This wealthy region, comprising much of what is called the Fertile Crescent, later became a valuable part of various Persian, Greek, and Roman empires. After the 7th century A.D., it became part of the Islamic world.

Historic Mesopotamia was ruled by great rulers such as Hammurabi, who was the first to codify the laws governing the life of its citizens, and King Nebuchadnezzar who established the Babylonian Empire. Tales of King Nebuchadnezzar, One Thousand and One Arabian Nights, Aladdin and his Magic Lamp, Sinbad the Sailor, and the songs of the Children of Israel by the rivers of Babylon remain with us to this day. It was the home of Abraham and Sarah before they moved to Hebron. Centuries before Christ, the Middle East was a center of advanced civilization, while many Europeans were still living in mud huts.

Iraq's capital, Baghdad, became the capital of the Abbasid Caliphate in the 8th century. A caliphate is the area ruled by the caliph, an Islamic spiritual leader. The Abbasids created a thriving culture that is called "The Golden Age of Islam." My distant relative Yahya was sent by the Abbasid rulers of Baghdad to teach the Koran in the village of Ana, just south of my hometown Rawa. Ana, a city founded millennia before the time of Nebuchadnezzar, was on the main road connecting Baghdad to Syria. Centuries later it would serve as one of the seats of eastern Christianity, serving Persian Christians. Such is the mosaic historical pattern of my homeland.

My distant ancestor, Yahya, later moved on to a sparsely populated settlement just north of Ana. His hospitality was legendary. He was affectionately called Yahya al-Rawi, which translates as John the Water-bearer, as he would provide free water and lodging for the traders traveling from Syria further east or vice versa. Tradition is strong in our land, and this practice continues to the present day.

Iraq's history is marked with notable literary achievements. The Sumerians, considered one of the earliest world civilizations, were established in Mesopotamia over a thousand years before the Babylonians came on the scene in 2,000 B.C. The Sumerians are remembered for their contributions to the field of education. Both writing and the telling of time were invented by the Sumerians. They divided the circle into 360 degrees.

The ancients of Mesopotamia had great knowledge of medical science, architecture, metaphysics, and so on. Cuneiform, the first phonetic system of writing, was developed by the Mesopotamians and then introduced to the world. The world's first great masterpiece of literature was composed there. "The Epic of Gilgamesh" is the story of a prominent Assyrian king who sought to teach us the difference between wisdom and knowledge.

Modern Iraq came into being when Britain seized the

territory from Ottoman Turkey during World War I. Shortly afterward, in April 1920, the British Mandate of Mesopotamia was created under the authority of the League of Nations. On October 3, 1932, the kingdom of Iraq was granted independence. Various kings of the Hashemite tribe and others ruled Iraq until 1958 when the monarch was overthrown and the Republic of Iraq was created.

Saddam Hussein came into power in 1979 and ruled until the invasion of Iraq in 2003. Despite the negative aspects of his rule, under Saddam, Iraq grew to be a progressive and a leading country in the Arabic world. It had one of the strongest school systems in the Middle East. Saddam's endorsement of universal primary education, schooling for girls, and a secular academic curriculum won Iraq a UNESCO prize in 1982 for eradicating illiteracy. Its museums were amongst the finest in the world, and its prestigious universities were the pride of the Arabic world.

Iraq's geographical location, combined with abundant natural resources, makes it a strategically important place. In the southwest lies the heart of the country, partly desert with a broad fertile plain watered by the Tigris and Euphrates Rivers.

Western Iraq comprises a single large province, Anbar, located to the west of Baghdad. I, Mahmoud, was born into a loving close-knit family in the Anbar Province, in the town of Rawa, in late 1984. The Euphrates River represented the main line of communication in Anbar in the old days, with numerous towns and settlements lining its banks.

A part of our town juts out like a peninsula into the Euphrates River, making our land green and our air always fresh. The fields are a symphony of colors and overflowing with flowers in the spring. People from this town are known by the appellation *Rawi*, or surname *al-Rawi*, or the plural *Rawiyen* for those who live in Rawa.

Though we later moved to Baghdad when Dad died, most of our extended family still lives in Rawa. The people of Rawa see themselves as one big family, and many of us had exceptionally large families as well. My grandfather had seven brothers and four sisters, so I have many, many cousins!

Rawa is legendary for its hospitality, as in the past it graciously provided for travelers coming from Syria into Iraq. Salam al-Rawi, an acquaintance of my father, who ran the successful Moustache Restaurant in New York City, says, "If you're in Rawa and you ask for a hotel or a restaurant, the people smile because every single house is open to guests to eat and sleep."

Rawiyen refuse, to this day, to allow any restaurants or hotels, but rather insist on lodging and feeding visitors themselves. This habit was just a part of our ancient tribal culture that has remained until this day.

2

My Early Years

The Iran-Iraq War

I was the fifth child in our family. Little Mariam, the sixth, was born in late 1988. Dad, whom we lovingly called Abu, was an officer in Saddam's army and was off fighting in the Iran-Iraq War, an event which played out in the background of my earliest years. I was safe at home in our little town, yet not too far from home was a war so savage that it was later known as the bloodiest war in the Mideast since the Mongol invasion in the year 1200.

Linda and Rana were my older sisters by a few years. They loved to help Mom take care of me in their girlish ways. I always wanted to follow my brother Abdullah around. He was five years older than me and even sometimes included me in games with his friends. We played "Hide and Seek" in our neighborhood and "Ha'a," a fun game played with sticks and stones.

Our town Rawa, which is on the Euphrates River had water and plenty of it. We would love to play in the beautiful waters and go fishing for carp. We also would take trips to the nearby date palms. There were so many types of dates.

Grandpa would tell us tales of times past and about the neighborhood where he grew up, now under the Euphrates River due to a dam built upstream. He seemed to be sad when he told us about old Rawa, under water now due to "development."

Our town was like a big happy family, and we all could trace our ancestry back to one of the four sons of Yahya al-Rawi, the water bearer. We lived in a very harmonious micro-society. Everybody was a relative, and everyone cared for each other.

Mohammed, the eldest child in our family, was eleven years older than me. He was my "father figure" as Dad was off to war. Umm (Mom) was loving and yet strict and made sure we did all our studies and kept our religious duties. She was also a great cook and would later work in the kitchen of a popular restaurant in Baghdad. Because of mom's cooking skills, we all ate well.

But I am getting ahead of my story.

All my uncles and aunts had gone to university, and many had obtained their master's degrees in various fields. Dad's youngest brother obtained a PhD in medicine in the U.K. The majority of young people in our hometown Rawa not only graduated from college, but had master's degrees and many even PhDs. Our country was producing brilliant scientists, engineers, and poets. Many literary lights of the modern Arabic world came from Iraq. Abu—my dad, that is—studied Business Administration before he had become a soldier and went off to war against Iran.

There were few tensions in the home. Dad, when home, would sometimes get upset with his firstborn,

Mohammed, who was crazy about Michael Jackson's music at the time and would like to breakdance. Michael Jackson was "rocking the desert" from Iraq to Saudi Arabia and throughout North Africa. Breakdancing was the rage in Iraq in the mid-1980s, and alcohol was also flowing freely in Baghdad at the time. It seemed Iraq loved everything Western. Much to my mother's chagrin, Mohammed would even joke that he was "Mohammed Jackson."

Dad felt Iraq did not need all these outside cultural influences which he said were weakening the moral fibre of Iraq's ancient and glorious culture. He would say that many songs of the West carried a message contrary to Iraq's traditional values. Western culture was making great inroads into Iraqi society. The Baathist party, which ruled Iraq, suppressed Islam as a political force and tried to keep Iraq as a secular state which they felt would be the key to progress.

Though life in the town of Rawa was simple, the Middle East is quite complex, and it had been the complexities of the Middle East that had sent my father off to war with our neighbor Iran.

Our war with Iran, which started in September of 1980, was the beginning of more than four intense decades of suffering for the people of Iraq. The Iraqis became a people of sorrow, well-acquainted with grief.

We were not all aware that many events befalling us in the 1980s were being decided in the USA, a country far away, across a continent and an ocean. These decisions in faraway nations would profoundly affect our lives, and lead to the death of my father in a war that was largely produced by the interference of these western powers in the lands of the Middle East.

I learned later, while studying at Anbar University, how in 1953, British and U.S. intelligence services engineered a coup to overthrow the first democratically elected government in the Mideast—Mohammed Mossadeq, the elected leader of Iran. He had angered the West by taking control of the oil industry.

The West installed Mohammad Reza Shah Pahlavi, better known as the Shah of Iran, who ruled Iran with his savage secret police. We were at war with Iran when I was born. The U.S. support of the repressive regime of the Shah earned them the undying hatred of the millions of Iranians who  suffered from the barbaric treatment the Shah meted out to those who opposed him. For years the USA had sold billions of dollars' worth of weapons to the Shah government.

The callous behavior of the U.S.-backed Shah strengthened the Islamic fundamentalists in Iran who overthrew the Shah in 1979. Almost overnight, America's most trustworthy ally in the region became its sworn enemy. The mullahs who led the new revolutionary government in Iran, instead of emulating the West, completely rejected it along with everything modern. Soon afterwards, they declared their intent to spread their revolutionary Islamic fundamentalist gospel far beyond their borders to the oil-rich, but militarily weak, Gulf States.

The United States looked desperately for a new local strongman to use to contain Iran and found him in our present ruler, Saddam Hussein. They saw in Saddam the lesser of two regional evils, someone who might bring stability to the region. Saddam was to protect America's friends in the Gulf. The U.S. adopted as its policy a practice based on an old Arab adage which states, "The enemy of my enemy is my friend."

Saddam Hussein virtually owed his position and military strength to the Western coalition allies who a decade later were to be pitted in combat against him. Iraq became the largest importer of weapons in the world, financed largely by "generous donations" from the other oil-rich Gulf States who were eager to underwrite the cost of the war to contain Iran, but were unwilling to shed their own blood.

During the war, Iraq purchased over $40 billion worth of arms from the U.S., and we purchased American food at subsidized prices. Though America was helping us my father never trusted that the U.S. really had Iraq's interests at heart, and he was right in his suspicions.

At the same time, the Soviet Union sold or gave Iraq more military equipment and supplies than any other country. It is no wonder that Iraq built the fourth largest standing army in the world. Dad also disliked the Communist ideology Russia was promoting along with the armaments it was giving us and felt Iraq should be free from all foreign influences.

In 1986, some high-ranking American officials indulged in a sideshow of realpolitik that bewildered even seasoned masters of intrigue like Saddam. The Iran Contra affair, as it was called, involved high-ranking members of the Reagan Administration illegally selling arms to Iran. The proceeds from the sales were then used to purchase arms for the Nicaraguan Contras in a clandestine operation.

While this game of double-dealing was going on, sadly, tens of thousands of young Arabs and Persians were dying on the battlefield. After nearly eight years, the war with Iran came to a stalemate with over one million casualties on both sides.

The war resulted in many economic difficulties. We were looking forward to our father coming home and our life returning to normal. We all missed him. Mohammed, Mom, and even my sisters did small jobs to make ends meet for the family in Dad's absence.

Sadly, when Dad returned from the war it was in a body bag.

Less than two months before the war ended, Dad died while retaking Majnun Island from Iran in late June 1988. I was nearly four at the time. It was the beginning of many great sorrows that I would live through while growing up.

Dad's death tore our family apart. The grief was immense! Mom was shattered. She was six months pregnant when Dad died. Her tears were unstoppable. His last visit home had been memorable; he was extremely happy that the war was ending . . . and now a dark cloud hung over the family.

Although the faces of those in the procession to the mosque have blurred with time, I can still recall my

mother's wan face sharp with grief in starkly pale contrast
to her mourning dress, and the gloomy face of my brother.
Nine-year-old Abdullah had howled like a wolf on the day
the terrible news of father's death reached us. He bitterly
lamented because the foundation of his life had been torn
away from underneath him, stealing the very essence of
his childish world of safety.

Now the Earth was opening to receive our father, and with
the dull thud of every spade of yellow soil that landed on
father's body, Abdullah's face seemed to lose its inquiring
innocence. This was a grief he should have known when
he was sixty years old, seasoned with time and experience,
old and wise with sorrows. Though he was unable to voice
the overwhelm of emotions that flooded his young soul, a
darkness began to grow in his heart, a helpless anger
began to quietly boil like a steaming pool of mud that
would one day erupt like a geyser.

Grandfather said the prayers at Dad's funeral. The
memory burns vividly in my mind. Most of our extended
tribal family came to the funeral, including my favorite
uncle, Mustafa, a well-known musician in Iraq who
performed live on TV, at weddings, parties, and elsewhere.
Even as a little child, I remember how he would sing for us
on family get-togethers.

My brothers, Mohammed and Abdullah, were despondent
for months. It broke something in Abdullah. Mom tried
hard to cheer us all up.

It was arranged for our family to move to Baghdad where
Dad's brother Sami, a prominent engineer, could help
support the family. Mom was able to find work as a chef in
an upscale Baghdadi restaurant.

Shortly after moving to Baghdad, Mariam was born into the world already an orphan, into a grieving family, a city being drained of wealth and academics, and a country drumming with war talk. Being fatherless decreed her and all of us "orphans" in our culture—a child who has lost his father, the main breadwinner of the home. Mariam would never hear her father's voice and never feel his protective arm around her. She would never be fed by his hand in our joyful family feasts in Rawa.

Iraq was left with a foreign debt of more than $40 billion after the war with Iran. We were successful in limiting the expansion and influence of the Iranian brand of Islam into Iraq and the nearby Sunni States of Kuwait, Saudi Arabia, Jordan, and elsewhere. Yet Saudi Arabia, Kuwait, and our Arab neighbors in the Gulf would not financially recompense us for the great sacrifices we made to protect their lands from Iran. Saddam accused Kuwait of siphoning off millions of barrels of oil from an underground reservoir straddling our common border through the unlawful practice of slant-drilling.

This issue would be a contributing factor to more war and death in the following years.

3

Invasion of Kuwait

Dark Clouds on the Horizon

These were sad times for me and my family. Besides losing our beloved father, some of our acquaintances left Iraq during the war. Older brother Mohammed's favorite cousin, Johnnie, left Iraq five years earlier with his family and moved to Egypt. Johnnie was a Christian as one of dad's sisters had married a Chaldean Christian and Johnnie was their eldest child.

Chaldeans have been living in Mesopotamia since time immemorial and many of them are Christian. They speak a language related to Aramaic, the language of Jesus. Many Christians left Iraq during the long Iran-Iraq War and made their way to Jordan, Egypt, Sweden, and the USA.

Muslims and Christians lived in harmony during those days. The Iraqi Christian Church was one of the oldest churches in the world, having been established in Iraq nearly 2,000 years ago. Well over one million Christians worshipped freely in Iraq.

Christians rose to the top under Saddam Hussein, notably Deputy Prime Minister Tariq Aziz. The Baathist regime kept a lid on anti-Christian violence. Besides the

Chaldeans, another significant Christian community was the Assyrians, the descendants of the ancient empires of Assyria and Babylon. They embraced Christianity in the first century AD.

Grandfather had always taught us that the Christians were the nearest to Muslims in love and compassion.[2] Whether Christian, Muslim, or Jew, we all considered ourselves Iraqis and prided ourselves in our past, our education, and the number of scientists and doctors Iraq was producing.

Meanwhile, on the street there was a lot of resentment amongst ordinary Iraqis towards Kuwait and Saudi Arabia. We felt our wealthy Kuwaiti and Saudi neighbors should have been helping us more in carrying the financial burden of the war with Iran. We were not fairly reimbursed for the enormous sacrifice we had paid with the blood of hundreds of thousands of our young soldiers.

Kuwait, which we considered once part of Iraq, refused to pay for the losses we suffered in defending them. Iraqis believe that Kuwait was an artificial state created by Britain in the early 1920s. Severing the territorial entity, "Kuwait," from the rest of Iraq served to weaken Arab nationalism and block Iraqi access to the Persian Gulf.

Time is different in the Middle East. The events of post World War I still carried a bitter taste in the minds and hearts of many when the Arab nationalistic aspirations for freedom were largely ignored by the victorious allies. After WWI, the newly-formed League of Nations awarded Britain the mandates of Palestine, Transjordan (Jordan),

---

[2] The Quran. Al Ma'idah Surah 5:82.

and Iraq, while France was awarded Syria and Lebanon. Cooperative Arab sheiks were installed as monarchs and artificial borders were drawn up which largely ignored the wishes of the local population, resulting in many problems that still exist today.

Now, after the Iran war, Kuwait and Iraq were engaged in a war of words. After checking with the U.S., the lone superpower in the world at that time, and receiving American assurance that a border war with Kuwait would not affect Iraq's relations with America, Saddam Hussein invaded and occupied Kuwait in August 1990. The world was shocked.

Immediately after the Iraqi annexation of Kuwait in August 1990, the propaganda machine against Iraq went into full gear. Kuwait and Saudi Arabia spent millions paying public relations firms in the U.S. to convince America to go to war against Iraq. They even dared to have a young girl, Nayirah, who turned out to be the daughter of the Kuwaiti ambassador to the U.S., dramatically speak bold lies before the Congressional Human Rights Caucus on October 10, 1990, in order to convince them to go to war with Iraq. It would take years before the U.S. was willing to admit that this actually happened.

The temperature of Iraq is blistering hot in the summer, regularly reaching a scorching 110 degrees Fahrenheit, but this year we felt the heat in more ways than one with a major storm looming over the Iraqi annexation of Kuwait. The prospect of war struck fear into our hearts. Never could we imagine that this war on the horizon would lead to the death of more than a million Iraqis over the coming decades. We had just lost 500,000 Iraqi lives in the war with Iran and most of the common people did not want another war.

While many in the West were under the spell of Saudi Arabia's and Kuwait's propaganda machine influencing them to go to war, something else was taking place in Kuwait. Saddam's soldiers were not taking babies out of incubators and letting them die on the cold hospital floors as the daughter of the Kuwaiti ambassador in Washington had blatantly lied about before the Human Rights Caucus. In reality, his soldiers, amongst many other things, were liberating dozens of Filipino maidservants and others who had come to Kuwait to work, only to be made into sex slaves of their cruel Kuwait masters who held their passports and would not let them leave their villas!

Stories of the joyful liberation of these women seeped out into the world media, but they were quickly swept away under the mountain of lies and partial truths that Saudi Arabia financed. Their large public relations companies were superb at blurring the truth. Their sole aim was to convince America to go to war with Iraq and to defeat Saddam Hussein, who had threatened the lives of wealth and the status quo of the sheikdoms of the Arab Gulf states and the royal family of Saudi Arabia. It would take a quarter of a century until people in the West would begin to wake up to the realities of Saudi Arabia.[3]

---

[3] Saudi Arabia, similar to the Islamic state, ISIS, uses beheading as a means to punish criminals in their country, including those guilty of adultery, treason, gay sex, drug offences, sorcery, witchcraft, and apostasy.

Sad to say, Saudi Arabia, like the Islamic state, uses "beheadings" as a means of punishing criminals in their country, including those guilty of adultery, treason, gay sex, drug offences, sorcery, witchcraft, and apostasy.

Kuwait, like Saudi Arabia, was a brutal dictatorship, oppressing any dissenting voices, with the ruling elite kept in power by selling oil to the West. Dictators have been fairly common in the Middle East, and the Western nations tolerated the ones who gave them good oil benefits.

The powerful oil lobbies, armaments industries, and politicians would not let anything undermine the long term relationship of Saudi Arabia with the West. The bottom line was "we needed their oil," and nothing would ever be allowed to interfere with that, so the stage was set for war.

We felt helpless in Baghdad. Many with money and who were highly educated immediately sought employment outside of Iraq as the drums of war pounded louder. A coalition of hundreds of thousands of soldiers from distant lands was amassing in nearby countries to fight against us in Kuwait.

All across our neighborhood, windows were being boarded up in preparation for the coming war. I did not fully understand what was taking place. I was only six years old at that time and my world was vastly different. My world was school, homework, and the fun of marbles, football, hide-and-seek, and other games on the backstreets of Baghdad.

Nearly every afternoon I met my cousin Yusuf close to where we lived. In the yard of an abandoned building we played with our marbles, a treasure for kids our age. Yusuf was already eight years old. I liked him because he treated me like someone his age. He was gentle and had taught me many tricks and how to play games.

Yusuf had a friend, Badr. I didn't like it when he came to join us. He had also lost his father in the war with Iran. Yusuf said he had no mother either and lived with his old uncle.

Badr was a rough boy, loud and pushy. He couldn't stand to lose a game of marbles. One day he cheated so obviously and took most of Yusuf's marbles, put them in his pocket, and ran away.

I thought for sure Yusuf would never play with him again so I was incredibly surprised to see Badr appear again the next day. Yusuf had all the marbles Badr had taken away from him the day before.

We then played peacefully together. I think for the first time Badr didn't throw a fit when he lost. When I asked Yusuf later how he got his marbles back and why Badr was so nice, he said he had gone to Badr's house and had given him the best golden marble he had. Badr couldn't believe it. "Why do you do this to me?" he queried. "I don't want to lose my friend," Yusuf answered. Badr gave him all his marbles back. From that day on Badr never cheated again. I was struck by the kindness of Yusuf. It left a great impression on me.

While we were lost in our world of marbles and other games, the peoples of the world feared how big this war looming in the horizon might become, some even wondering if the "death of civilization" could happen in the same place where civilization began. Mohammed, now 17, was conscripted into the army and sent to the war zone in Kuwait.

At night, we would often hear mother in her room weeping. The joy we once knew in Rawa seemed distant in the fearful streets of Baghdad.

4

Gulf War I

Shooting Fish in a Barrel

America, the sole world "super" power at that time, was caught in the Saudi/Kuwaiti financed war propaganda, and immediately voted to go to war against Iraq. It was not until years later that various official agencies admitted that they were strongly influenced and sometimes deceived by the intense war-promoting, anti-Saddam media barrage at that time.

By November 1990, the UN Security Council had authorized the use of "all necessary means" of force against Iraq if it did not withdraw from Kuwait by the 15th of January 1991. Saddam did not comply with the request of the UN. Many Arab nations chose to join in the war against Saddam. We were isolated.

And so began the First Gulf War. From the 17th of January 1990 to the 23rd of February 1991, for 42 days and nights bombing air raids consisting of 100,000 sorties (air missions), 2,400 sorties a day, 100 per hour, one sortie every 40 seconds rained hell down upon Iraq in the form of 88,500 tons of bombs dropped on us. Our entire military and civilian infrastructure were destroyed. It was the beginning of the era of systematic strategic bombing. Things would never be the same again.

The war of 1991 to liberate Kuwait from Iraq would eventually be called the first Gulf War. The war set off a series of events that would lead to the death of over 1 million Iraqis in the coming 25 years. While George Bush spoke about a new world order ushering in an era of peace envisioned by the United Nations, horrors upon horrors would continue year after year, and it would result in Iraq, decades later, being partially controlled by America's arch-rival Iran. The intervention of the U.S. into Iraqi affairs became totally meaningless. Thousands of American soldiers would die in future Middle East wars that profited nothing, and these soldiers' efforts to bring a change to Iraq were in vain.

Operation Desert Storm was the name given to the U.S.-Allied war. It was a nightmare to live through. Endless bombing raids were raining fire on our land. It was impossible to sleep or live.

Mariam was two years old when the bombs rained down day and night. She was most afraid at night, her large brown eyes round with terror. Abdullah would sit with her on her soft blanket, her small young hand in his hand, He would teach her to laugh at the sound of explosions. She nestled her face in his shirt and felt safer somehow.

The aerial bombardment of Iraq was on a scale that the world had never seen before. The Allies were, under the guise of implementing U.N. resolutions, pursuing an agenda to systematically destroy the entire Iraqi economic infrastructure. The aim was to so devastate Iraq that it would never again be a threat to the world's oil supply or to another key Western ally in the region—Israel. Saddam was outspokenly anti-Israel and was considered one of the most powerful enemies of the State of Israel.

Saddam's army did not stand a chance against the armies of the world that came against them. The war became very personal for me and my family when my oldest brother, Mohammed, was conscripted and sent to fight, even though he detested war and what it stood for. Mohammed would have preferred to stay home and hang out in the bars of Baghdad enjoying its vibrant nightlife. He had developed strong convictions that there must be a peaceful solution to conflicts, yet he obeyed his orders and joined the troops in Kuwait. There was a great amount of worry and concern in our family for Mohammed.

My mother wept over his conscription and departure; she who had already experienced the bitterness of war in the loss of her husband and father of her children. "What terrible, terrible things wars are," she said. "How can soft flesh fight cruel steel?" True, there are no winners in a war. It seems like mothers truly understand the real cost of war.

All of us lose in a war in one way or another. Mothers lose their boys; we lose our brothers; our countries lose governments and economies. The victors who win often win only to fight yet another day in another place.

Our personal family somehow survived the inhumane

systematic bombing of our country. It was not easy. Abdullah was my fierce defender during the frightful bombing of Baghdad. Despite our mother's protests, sometimes we would sneak out to play, and I always followed, cheerfully shadowing my big brother anywhere. The local toy shop sold mostly toy guns, but we were not permitted to play with them by mother, so we improvised, mostly playing soldiers with the other boys in burnt-out cars. The "bad guy" sitting in the front seat and others with black socks on their faces represented the police.

During the war, the neighborhood boys played little else, saw little else, except the piles of rubbish, the smoldering bomb craters, the ruined buildings and burning trash that littered the streets puddled with sewage water. We all especially liked to watch the noisy column of military vehicles rolling by, until one day, excited by the commotion and oblivious to the danger, I leaned out too far from the curb and almost fell in front of the treads of a tank. Horrified, Abdullah, ever watchful, snatched me back by my shirt just in time. He dared not tell our mother, but we did not venture out for days afterwards.

At home, Mother often sang songs to try and keep a positive environment in the home. She kept clothes, milk and blankets in our basement shelter in case of emergencies. I still remember today the comforting warmth and clean smell of my quilted orange blanket. While we huddled together, Abdullah and I would play marbles or knucklebones under the blankets with a torch to pass the time. We would laugh and talk. Under our blankets we were invincible.

Auntie Kausar, whose husband was off in Kuwait, pleaded

with us to come to the Amiriyah shelter because the bombing had greatly intensified in the past week. She said it was too dangerous where we lived as we were too close to the industrial centers that were being targeted. The Amiriyah shelter was considered to be so strong that it could survive a nuclear blast.

We were hesitant to move there as the shelter was crowded and Mom, for some reason, did not feel fully safe, and she did not want to subject little Mariam to more change. We did not want to leave our little basement shelter. Mom's hesitancy saved her and our lives.

On the afternoon of February 12th, Mom visited Kausar and her family, bringing some gifts and supplies. It was my cousin Salih's birthday. That would be the last time we would see them as the following morning at 4:30 a.m., two stealth bombers dropped one ton laser-guided bombs on the shelter. It was a hideous, bloody massacre—408 women and children died in the shelter. The fire from the bombing was so intense it even melted the metal of the shelter.

The next day relatives sobbed helplessly as rescue workers brought out bodies—most of them mangled, some beyond recognition, some still smoldering—from the bombed-out shelter. Even the media was overcome with grief. It was too grim to film. Mom, overwhelmed by the sight, fell to the ground in uncontrollable sorrow.

Since we had moved to Baghdad, Kausar was always there

helping us. Abdullah, who was only thirteen, was in the center of things, pulling out bodies, rescuing some. Many bodies were just piled onto the back of a truck. Sadly, Kausar and her children were among these. Mom had to identify them. We buried Kausar and the mangled, charred bodies of all her children.

Years later, I again visited the Amiriyah Shelter. It is one of the most haunting things I have ever seen. I could still see the fingernail marks on the blood stained walls as people tried to escape. Events like these are what fueled the hate and wrath of extremists like ISIS. It does not excuse the atrocities of ISIS, but it does help explain them.

Two weeks later, our soldiers began to leave Kuwait, but sad to say, our worst fears for Mohammed came to pass. The allied forces that confronted Saddam's forces in Kuwait quickly overcame them. Despite Saddam's bold and foolish talk, our armies were powerless against the host of countries arrayed against us.

Mohammed retreated, along with the other hundreds of thousands of soldiers fleeing Kuwait, to the perceived safety of Basra. It was late February 1990, U.S. spokesperson Marlin Fitzwater had stated that the U.S. and its coalition partners would not attack Iraqi forces leaving Kuwait. The Iraqi army, in an agreement with the U.S., was leaving Kuwait and traveling on the lone desert highway to Basra when the nightmare began.

Unbeknownst to our soldiers on the ground, American generals, like little boys with firecrackers, were testing the power of their new weapons. American forces had a sitting target. Saddam's army was like "fish in a tank" as one general boasted. Plane after plane bombed our retreating soldiers. There were so many planes striking the fleeing army, pilots said, that the "killing box" had to be divided in half by air traffic controllers to prevent mid-air collisions. The ruthless bombing went on for hour upon hour leaving everything in its path burnt to a crisp. Even soldiers fleeing into the desert were incinerated.

After more than 36 hours of this relentless bombing of our fleeing soldiers, George Bush Sr. was sickened and repulsed when he saw the videos and gave the order to stop the slaughter. Witnesses of the attack were struck by the scale of its destruction and the one-sidedness of the bombing.

The result was tens of thousands of charred Iraqi soldiers and civilians. Time Magazine, in its March 18, 1991 issue, wrote: "On the inland highway to Basra is mile after mile of burned, smashed, shattered vehicles of every description—tanks, armored cars, trucks, autos, fire trucks . . ." The inhumane destruction littered the highway from Kuwait City to Basra. The generals, and those who produce weapons, were gloating. War had been good for the economy and new weapons had been tested. Kuwait was liberated at the cost of over $60 billion.

Of course, I did not know all this at the time, but later as a young teen I devoured history and whatever I could read about world events. I wanted to know why this mighty power would destroy most of my family, my country, and attempt to wipe our civilization off the face of the earth.

Some of my friends whose fathers or brothers were lost in the war were able to bury their dead. Our family would never know this simple joy or comfort. Mohammed died during this terrible slaughter. My brother's remains must have been beyond recognition. He was just another of the many soldiers whose bodies were incinerated in this massive firebombing.

The pain and grief in our family was unbearable. There was no funeral to be held for Mohammed, no way of knowing anything about his remains. He was reduced to a scorched skeleton, part of the charcoaled dust on the burnt-out landscape that would soon be called the "Highway of Death."

Linda, Rana, and Abdullah were despondent and shell-shocked. Though I was only seven, I remember this time well, though I did not understand until much later how deeply it affected Abdullah. I did sense though that his childish joy was being snuffed out. He was only thirteen. I can still visualize the way he would weep…"How could America do this to us? Dad had died fighting Iran, the country that held Americans captive for so long. Now our oldest brother is dead. Which side is America on?"

We had considered ourselves friends of America. Saddam, like the United States, believed in a secular state. Abdullah was never the same. The death of my beloved father and now my brother left a great emptiness in my heart, too.

Those fragile early years of childhood that should have been sheltered and carefree were not for Abdullah. He was one of those children who could listen at doors, unnoticed by grownups, so was able to give an accurate profile of all the world's leaders and the current state of war and politics in our country to our little neighborhood band of boys. He could lip read adult's whisperings and hovered near the unemployed men sipping coffee, smoking shisha pipes, and talking about the war in a nearby cafe. He had a curious mind and heard and understood the reports of indiscriminate bombings going on in our country. He witnessed the anger, the despair, the deprivation, the hunger, and the grief of many families. These were the unseen wounds shaping Abdullah's tender soul, forming his character, filling his memories, and leading him to the inevitable choices on the path that lay ahead of him.

The slaughter of the retreating Iraqi army on the Basra highway was recorded as a victorious day for the American Republic. But in reality, it was yet another massacre in their long history of expanding their massive empire at the expense of subjugating other peoples.

We all know that 80% of the Native American population died during the founding of the American Empire. Hundreds of thousands of Africans were brought to America to work in the fields and build their country. In the Filipino-American War, the U.S. justified the brutal killing of the Philippine people by telling their soldiers that the Filipinos were not humans, but half-monkey. Now they were demonizing us just the same.

Every time the word Muslim or Islam was used in the Western media, they had a negative adjective alongside it. "Muslim terrorism," "Islamic extremism," and "radical Islam" were amongst the dozens of words they used to make an entire population of people fearful of anything connected with Islam.

In the late American President Eisenhower's own words, the U.S. built a "military-industrial complex" of massive proportions, greater than the budgets of entire nations. How stupid Saddam was to think he could fight this seemingly invincible power.

Many people believe that the first Gulf War, and the ferocity with which the Allies waged it, were intentionally escalated well beyond what the United Nations resolutions provided for, and that such mass destruction had never been imagined or approved by the United Nations Security Council. By the end of the war, very few people felt that the objective of the Allies was to simply enforce the Security Council resolutions concerning Kuwait.

The loss of my big brother Mohammed was my second deep sorrow as a young child. Mohammed was an idol to me. He was like a father after my dad had passed away. I so much wanted to be like Mohammed, and now he is gone.

How fast the world can change.

Mom was in such great depression and sorrow. All the cheers of sending the soldiers off to war were now gone. All the glory and the glamour of marching off to war as the people cheer them is now hushed. There they lie, silently, charred beyond recognition on the highway of death, and nobody cheers anymore, nobody cares, so few even remember.

Our uncle, Sami, would curse the politicians and bureaucrats and munitions makers, the warmongers and the people who want the wars but never have to fight them; people who want the wars to save their businesses and their political parties but don't have to fight them themselves. Uncle Sami, like many Iraqis, was mad at the world, at life. It had been over a decade of war now for the Iraqis.

The one bright spot of that year was the continued

cheerfulness of my youngest sister Mariam whose smile lit up the darkest nights of the war. She seemed oblivious to the terrors taking place around her and was innocently unaware of what lay ahead.

5

Devastation of Economic Sanctions

They died silently, humanity had closed its ears to their cry.

—Khalil Gibran Khalil

"Sabah al khair," may the morning be full of goodness, was the usual cheerful greeting of Mariam every morning as she joined us at the breakfast table. We would reply in unison, "Sabah an Noor," may the morning be bright with light! Though things were difficult, Mom would try to make breakfast special so we could have a good start to our days. Abdullah and I were treated exceptionally well at home, being the only remaining men in our immediate family. Mom and our sisters spoiled us.

Linda and Rana were always helping mom in the kitchen, as traditionally in the Middle East girls help the mothers at home. Our breakfast meals were great, with cheese, eggs, jam, molasses, dates, and our traditional pita bread. Abdullah and I would sometimes go with our cousins to pick the dates. Our stomachs were filled from snacking on the sweet, sticky fruit by the time we brought the full baskets home for our families. Mom would often make Madgooga by pounding dates and sesame seeds together by hand, making the world's oldest energy bar.

After Mohammad's death, we had hoped life may finally return to normal. I was starting 2nd grade. Linda and Rana went to the same school. Abdullah was entering high school, and Uncle Sami helped him with his tuition to Baghdad College, an elite secondary school for boys aged 11 to 18 in Baghdad. It was initially a Catholic school, originally founded and operated by American Jesuits. With the secularization of Iraq over time the nature of the school had changed from the days of its Jesuit founders, but it still had an interesting blend of Muslim, Christian, and Jewish students.

In the tumultuous times that followed the first Gulf War, Saddam quickly went about rebuilding his army and trying to restore order as best as he could. His efforts to rebuild the country, though, favored his army and those around him. It seemed he had become somewhat oblivious to the suffering of many of the common Iraqi people.

It was about this time that America and the Western nations imposed crippling sanctions upon Iraq that would eventually lead to the death of well over 100 Iraqi children every day. Iraq hoped for more leniency when Bill Clinton was elected president in 1992, but their hopes were dashed with the continuance of the economic embargo and the quiet war President Clinton continued to carry out on the country, dropping countless bombs on us during his eight-year presidency.

Clinton used the sanctions as a tool in his attempt to remove Saddam Hussein from power, but the effects of the sanctions were catastrophic. Iraq experienced shortages of food, medicine, and clean drinking water. There was an increase in cancer in the years following the war, and my little sister Mariam was one of the many children who fell ill with this condition.

There was widespread malnutrition. Due to the crippling economic sanctions children could not obtain the medicines and nourishing food needed to stay healthy. We prayed and prayed for Allah to grant Mariam healing, but she only grew worse. We could not understand why the Western nations in their attempt to bring about regime change were punishing ordinary Iraqi citizens.

The doctors held out little hope for Mariam's survival. "She will either die before the end of the year or she will live and grow up stunted and with low intelligence," the doctor told us. "It is not just the lack of medicines. Due to the embargo we are not receiving new-generation drugs, advances in medicine, science, food, anything."

As the years passed by, our economic situation deteriorated due to the economic sanctions. I remember going hungry many nights. It seemed like only yesterday we were enjoying Mom's great meals. I would dream of the better days back in Rawa, longing to be a child again, far from the terrors of Baghdad. Malnutrition among children under five was consistently over 25%. The entire social fabric of Iraq was torn apart by these cruel economic sanctions. Sad to say, several anti-government protests were brutally suppressed by Saddam Hussein during this time.

During the day Mariam was lovingly cared for by our female relatives while Mama worked. It was in those long, hot Baghdad evenings that she would often keenly feel her mother's absence and whimper for her tender embrace and gentle voice. Then Linda and Rana would carry her through the streets that often rumbled with military vehicles to watch Mama work through the gleaming windows of the restaurant. She worked hard, preparing lamb kebabs on long steel prongs, grilled fish, freshly caught in the ancient river Tigris, steaming bowls of biryani, the rice yellowed by the turmeric and flecked with almonds, raisins and spices, and platters piled with colorful vegetables for the guests. The sights made their stomachs ache, and she was occasionally permitted to meet them at the back door with small parcels of warm rice, topped with a few tasty morsels.

Mariam had a tea set made from cardboard scraps. The saucers were decorated with red flowers drawn by her sisters. She would sit in the shade of the date palms on the cobblestones pretending to have feasts with her doll, using grass and dandelions. Once Abdullah kicked them over, his resentment and frequent hunger often bubbled over into anger. I shouted at him. Grandpa always said to use words to settle quarrels, not fists. I felt bad for shouting and letting my anger get the better of me.

Mariam grew increasingly ill, her cancer, malnutrition, and frequent respiratory infections sapped her strength. When she could no longer play, we read to her. Books, at least, were plentiful in our humble home. I often would weep bitterly at night thinking of my little sister, Mariam. Would I also die, too, like her? Would I have anyone near to me when I died? Would I be surrounded by loved ones?

In her seventh winter, before she had begun to read, Mariam died.

We buried her within 24 hours. I tucked her small ragdoll and favorite picture book into her cold stiffening little hands. Then they wrapped her little thin figure in her funeral cloth. Her uncles and grandfather buried her in the chilled earth before the next sunset, long before spring.

Mariam never experienced a normal childhood. She did not know the joys many children experience. For most of her brief life, she only knew the severe sanctions that deprived her short childhood of the vital food and medicine that might have saved her.

Mother's sorrow caused her to nearly go insane. Our little cousin Eyman also died in the same hospital. She looked like one of the starving children in Africa. The images of Mariam and Eyman withering away due to lack of good food and medicine haunted my mind every waking hour.

Once again, our family was torn apart as life continued to be a nightmare after nightmare. Our memories of the past were now only painful ones. The present was miserable. Little did we know that this was child's play compared to what was to come.

Linda and Rana went into a deep sadness. No matter what games or fun things Abdullah and I tried to do, it seemed we could not find out how to release them from their prison of sorrow. In reality, we could not find a way to wipe the tears from all our hearts that were weeping.

Many nations expressed their concern over the alarming death rate of the children of Iraq. Dennis Halliday, the former U.N. humanitarian coordinator, bitterly observed that by his estimates over one million Iraqis had died, 500,000 of them being children.

These statistics on the rate of child mortality in Iraq were put to the U.S. Secretary of State Madeleine Albright in 1996 by Lesley Stahl of CBS News, posing the question, "We have heard that half a million children have died. I mean, that's more children than died in Hiroshima. And, you know, is the price worth it?"

Albright coldly replied, "I think this is a very hard choice, but the price—we think the price is worth it."

One U.N. worker after another resigned after seeing what the sanctions were doing to the Iraqi people. The world was aghast at such merciless diplomacy from the nations imposing these crippling sanctions on the common people. Dennis Halliday resigned from the organization in protest after spending a little over a year as the U.N. Humanitarian Coordinator in Iraq. He said the sanctions constituted genocide.

The real casualties of these unending sanctions were those who could least afford to pay the price or raise their voices to be heard, as in the case of little Mariam. Which poses the greater danger to the West's "vital regional interests" in the future?—The survival of Saddam Hussein or a generation of Iraqis made bitter by the indifference of Western nations which were raging unending war on Iraq?

By the time I was eleven, several of my best friends at school had somehow moved to other countries. If you had money or connections, you could make it to Jordan. After Dad's and Mohammed's deaths, we had neither. It seemed like mostly the hardened were left at school. Bullies often dominated the neighborhoods now. The lights of Iraq were being slowly extinguished.

Abdullah grew further withdrawn and strangely silent except for his occasional outbursts. He was a young teen now, angry and desperately looking for a way to take revenge on those who killed all that he held dear.

The rest of us were constantly hungry and did whatever we could to make money while trying to study and stay alive. My two older sisters, Linda and Rana, began helping mom at the restaurant. I poured myself into my studies, especially English language. I needed to understand the mind of these governments who were committing a silent genocide in our land.

Sure our country was not perfect, and many in our extended family did not support Saddam, including Uncle Salam who was living in the USA. I was not even a teen, but I knew enough to know that what was happening to our country, our people, our children, was wrong—terribly wrong. I couldn't understand why other countries didn't seem to care, didn't come to help us.

It was only later that I would learn that there were a few brave voices who stood up against the suffering we were enduring from these crippling sanctions.

6

Gulf War II

Shock and Awe

In 2000 newspapers announced that another Bush had
been elected president of the U.S. He was the son of the
man who slaughtered our soldiers and bombed our cities
without mercy back in 1991, yet who had been frustrated
in his ultimate goal of removing the Iraqi President
Saddam Hussein from power. My relatives said they could
see revenge written on his son's face, and worried that
around the corner worse days were coming.

For us, the election of George W. Bush was not a good
omen. We had considered his father as a modern day
crusader. Crusaders in the Middle East are remembered as
cruel invaders with a legacy of killing and destruction.

Then, in September 2001, the Twin Towers fell in New
York. The news said that Muslim extremists had attacked
America. Some Iraqis felt a twinge of joy to see the United
States experiencing a bit of the suffering she had meted out
upon us and others throughout the world. But most were
sad and had a sense of foreboding that this would be
blamed on us, even though Saddam was a Baathist trying
to maintain a secular society. Saddam had fought for years

against these same Muslim extremists who were now being accused of hijacking the four planes that hit the Towers in America.

On 9/11 Mom visited some Americans living close to the restaurant to offer her condolences. This happened throughout the Muslim world. Despite what governments say and do, my mom felt that the heart of the common people is the same all over the world and we all want peace and a better world for our children.

There were foreign Christian aid workers in Baghdad and other parts of Iraq during the difficult times of economic sanctions between the first and second Gulf Wars. They helped our sick in the hospitals and brought needed medicines, milk, and other items. Saddam's government allowed Christian aid workers to work freely throughout the country in those days, and to show the popular Gospel of Luke movie in schools and centers.

I was 13 when I saw the movie. It followed stories from the Book of Luke in the Bible. Afterwards, we had earnest discussions about when Jesus would return to put an end to the "Kiyamet" (Armageddon) our country was suffering. Jesus is highly respected in Islam and we were thankful for these visiting Christians from abroad who brought us much-needed supplies.

Somehow, even though Saddam had nothing to do with 9/11, America decided to attack Iraq and pressured other countries to join in the attack. "Shock and Awe" was the term used for this war, like a catchy phrase, not even considering the hundreds of thousands of innocents whose lives would be torn apart by the bombs and destruction. At this time there were rumors that Saddam was developing weapons of mass destruction, even though the U.N. inspectors said that there was no evidence of this.

Sad to say, the world has a short memory. As in the first Gulf War, armed with evidence based on fabrications and misinformation, President Bush was able to once again convince America to go to war. Bush and Blair, the Prime Minister of the U.K., had to come up with new reasons for overthrowing Saddam, and conveniently used the fabrication of "weapons of mass destruction." The mantra of "Iraq possessing weapons of mass destruction" was broadcast non-stop on the Western world's media outlets.

In reality Saddam was desperate to avoid war. Our country had suffered too much, and many children were suffering from malnutrition and a wide variety of illnesses. This was a time for peace, so our Christian Foreign Minister Tariq Aziz went on a diplomatic offensive appealing to the Pope and others.

Hope was being born in me again. Surely Tariq Aziz could convince the Christian West not to attack the suffering Iraqi people once more. I knew that Jesus said to "love your enemies," and I hoped he would be successful in his mission for peace.

Tariq Aziz also traveled to Assisi, Italy, in hopes of reminding the Christian world of the message of Saint Francis, who embodied peace and whose words "where there is hatred, let me show love" were known by so many. Proud Saddam, the great leader, took a very humble step and went to the extreme of publicly destroying his own missiles to show he was sincere in seeking peace. We did not want war. The essence of the Koran is peace; the root word of Islam is peace. We were seeking peace; we were tired of war.

My older brother Abdullah, now 24, wanted to join the resistance that was being organized to wage a guerilla war against a possible American occupation of Iraq. Mom begged him not to and made him promise not to use a weapon. She reminded him that our prophet Mohammed taught to "warn the killer that eventually he will be killed,"[4] and that "he who lives by the sword dies by the sword."

Grandpa was a big influence on us. He had a serenity about him that one day justice would reign and that through these dark hours, when the Muslims are being tested, that from these present ashes would spring forth the glorious age of Islam. He would remind us that the Koran, Surat Ash-Shura, verse 40, says, "The repayment of a bad action is one equivalent to it. But if someone pardons and puts things right, his reward is with Allah."

At the mosque, the Muslim Brotherhood told Grandpa that in three months we would have our freedom. America would remove Saddam Hussein and leave the Iraqi people in power and free to rule themselves. Grandfather seemed to be able to see into the future and told them that America would never willingly leave Iraq. He believed they would be here to stay.

The war began in March 2003. Ominous signs appeared at the outbreak of the war. A massive desert storm delayed

---

[4] From the Hadith; a collection of the sayings of the Prophet Mohammed, arranged in six canonical collections. The hadith are widely accepted by Sunni Muslims.

the attacks for a day. News outlets published photographs showing what appeared to be grotesque formations in the clouds, while others claimed they were heavenly appearances.

Whatever comfort or fear these gave, the first bombs brought everyone back to the brutal reality that our country was now entering another terrible war, one that would ultimately last from March 20, 2003 to December 2011. Eight years of war would leave Iraq further broken and destroyed, so weakened that afterward we could not protect ourselves from ISIS when they rose to power.

Despite the frequent bombing going on around us, life had to go on. My mom was able to continue her job at the restaurant. My sister Linda became old enough to work there too, which was helpful as it brought in more income to feed the remaining members of our family. My other sister Rana stayed home with me, and we did our best to keep up with our studies so that we could finish high school.

The 8th of April 2003 started like any other day. Mom and Linda left for the restaurant, Rana and I were at home, and Abdullah was out. Mom and Linda worked all morning at the restaurant preparing the lunch meals. After the midday cleanup was finished, it was their break time. As was their usual routine, they walked around the corner to the home of Mom's good friend Sana to drink tea and chat together with her and her two daughters. It was like an oasis of refreshment for Mom, sitting with her kind and longtime friend on the balcony, away from the work and pressures, and away from her memories of Mariam. Linda was a good friend of Sana's daughters, too, and they always found much to talk and laugh about despite the hardships of their young lives. Abdullah had also dropped by for a few minutes, to have a quick visit and a cup of tea, before heading on his way. Then it happened.

While lifting a cup of sweet Iraqi tea to her lips, mom breathed her last breath. Satellite-guided bombs moving at 900 mph, dropping from American fighter jets flying at 20,000 feet, suddenly rained down on them. After a three-second interval, two more 2,000-pound bombs were dropped. All hell had broken loose.

The Americans were aiming at the restaurant around the corner where Mom worked. Saddam Hussein was expected to be there for a private late lunch, and the laser-guided missiles were programmed accordingly. Instead, the precision-guided missiles destroyed the nearby homes of civilians who had nothing to do with the war or the Iraqi government, some of whom were pro-American. One of those three houses destroyed was Sana's house. There was a jagged crater about 25 feet deep, strewn with debris and body parts. Around the corner, the al-Sa'ah Restaurant had its windows blown out, leaving the clientele and staff bloodied, injured, and in a state of shock.

Abdullah had just left but was still close enough to be injured by the blast. Covered with blood and hysterical, he went out to try to find his mother and sister Linda. They were not alive when he found them. Words cannot describe what he saw and found.

And so, at the age of 18, I lost my mother and my older sister Linda. My eldest brother Mohammed had died on the retreat to Basra during the first war, my darling little sister Mariam left us during the economic sanctions, my father died when I was a wee child and now my mom and older sister were gone. I knew their bodies had been blown apart by 2,000 pound bombs, and I tried not to think about it. I felt like I had been blown apart too. How could I go on anymore? I was shattered. My world was destroyed beyond repair.

It would take years to come out of the deep depression I fell into. I wept for days and no longer wanted to live. Mom had been so proud of me. I would be graduating from my high school, Baghdad College, next month and was about to go off to university. I would have neither father nor mother at my graduation ceremony nor to help me face the world.

Only Rana and I remained at home, seeking answers to all the madness. There were no explanations available. We knew that war was absolute hell and that there had to be a better solution. We questioned why God would tear our family apart like this. We found comfort in the story of Job and others who had lost everything, and somehow we kept our faith in God.

Abdullah left home to join the resistance full-time. His way of dealing with his pain and anger was to take vengeance on those who he held responsible for the deaths of five members of our immediate family. By now, Abdullah had become quite radicalized. He railed about how the founding Americans had decimated the Native American population; imported slaves to increase their wealth; dropped the first atomic bomb in the history of mankind; and now were killing thousands of innocent civilians in our country. He felt completely justified in joining the fight against those he perceived as the enemies of his people and his family.

Back at home, Rana and I wondered if the American public really knew what was happening on the ground here, and if they did, why would they support this war? Many other innocent civilians died as Mom and Linda did. Over the course of the war many bombs "accidentally" killed thousands of civilians who happened to be near the explosions but killed none of the Iraqi leaders they were intended for.

The day following Mom and Linda's deaths, April 9, 2003, Saddam Hussein's government was toppled and lost control of Baghdad. U.S. forces had advanced into the center of the capital. In a symbolic moment, American soldiers helped a crowd of cheering Iraqis pull down a huge statue of the ousted president.

They were happy to see Saddam removed from power. Many young people wanted to see a change in Iraq, but the methods the West used to bring "democracy" to Iraq would only cause decades of confusion and turmoil. Parts of our country had been pushed back to the Stone Age. This was "liberation"?

On May 1, 2003, President George Bush declared "mission accomplished" in Iraq. It wasn't. In the months that followed, political grievances erupted into sectarian insurgencies across the country as Sunni and Shiite militias fought for power among themselves and against the U.S. troops who they regarded as "occupiers." Sad to say, Iraqi civilians bore the brunt of this turmoil. "Mission Accomplished" opened up a Pandora's Box of evil that would engulf our entire country and beyond for many years.

Three weeks later, the U.N. lifted economic sanctions on Iraq and gave its backing to the U.S.-led administration. With the lifting of sanctions, we could get needed medicines again and basic food items that had been difficult to purchase, but it was too late for our family, too late for Mariam.

Nevertheless, there was a glimmer of hope. Perhaps life would improve and things would get better again?

7

Tortured

The Nightmare of Abu Ghraib Prison[5]

Abdullah and several of his friends were arrested shortly after Mom's death and were taken to the infamous Abu Ghraib prison just outside of Baghdad where the scandals of Americans abusing Iraqi prisoners would soon shock the world. Abdullah was protesting the American presence in Iraq when he was arrested.

In prison, he was abused and terrorized by his American captors. It wasn't until nearly a year later that a series of photographs emerged showing some U.S. military personnel abusing Iraqi detainees at the Abu Ghraib prison. The scandal contributed to a major backlash against the United States and its forces. The graphic images show naked inmates being terrorized by dogs, prisoners stripped naked, piled into a grotesque human

---

[5] Chapter 7 may not be for everyone. You can skip over the torture of the prisoners in Abu Ghraib. However, it is important to know that Abu Ghraib was not the only prison where such treatment of prisoners took place. When I told this story in Romania, and later elsewhere, many people had a hard time believing this actually happened. It's a story that must be told.

pyramid and coerced to simulate indecent acts. Often, they were taunted by female soldiers. This went against the very essence of our culture.

The photos sparked a temporary outrage but were soon forgotten and Abdullah said not much changed; the guards were just more careful when they abused the prisoners. The psychological scars left on the Iraqi prisoners would last for a lifetime. The shame of being paraded naked caused more than a few prisoners to commit suicide after leaving the prison. It was impossible for an Iraqi man to face one's friends again after being sexually abused by his captors. "They would do the interrogations while I was naked, with a black bag over my head. I felt like I had completely lost control, that I was just some creature in their hands," said Salah al-Ejaili, former Abu Ghraib detainee. The torture and humiliation were worse than death.

The violations of human rights that Abdullah witnessed included physical and sexual abuse, torture, rape, sodomy, and murder. The unnervingly Christ-like photo of Ali Shallal Al Qaisi standing on a box while hooded, holding electrical cables became world famous. Most of the perpetrators of these crimes received only a reprimand. An internal investigation by the U.S. military in April 2004 described "sadistic, blatant and wanton criminal abuses" inflicted on detainees. The ramifications of the so-called "enhanced interrogation" methods used by the U.S. are still being felt today, not least by those tortured Iraqis who still live with post-traumatic stress disorder.

When we could visit Abdullah, we could see he was extremely traumatized and deeply wounded inside. He did not want to talk. Unbeknownst to most of the world, Abu Ghraib, though certainly the most notorious prison, was not the only one, and some would argue not even the worst. Most of the prisoners in these prisons were civilians, many of whom had been picked up in random military sweeps and at highway checkpoints. 90% of those held were later found innocent.

According to the Geneva Convention, occupying powers must bring safety and security to the civilians in the area it occupies. We thought maybe we could have freedom and security after two decades of suffering. How wrong we were.

My sister Rana and I would talk long hours about the events of our country. Rana had just turned 21 at the start of the second Gulf war. She was strikingly beautiful despite not wearing a smile. It should have been a happy time in her life. She could not talk long without breaking into tears. She would often tell me her memories of Dad. She was only six when he passed away. She had memories of Mohammed who died three short years later, and of Mariam who died during the economic crisis. Then, when she was about to celebrate her 21st birthday, Mom, the rock of our family, and Linda, who was about to be married, were horribly killed, two of the many innocents

America felt could be sacrificed in their pursuit of Saddam Hussein. I could not help Rana out of her sorrow as I was in such a deep state of depression myself.

The lights of our world were flickering out. Like Abdullah, I no longer had a reason to live and considered joining him in the growing insurgency against the American occupation. Yet, I feared if I died, who would care for Rana and keep our family legacy alive. Grandpa and Mom had always taught me to seek peaceful solutions to conflicts, and I tried to hold on to this belief, though the desire for revenge was drowning out the voice of peace within me.

On one of my visits to see Abdullah in Abu Ghraib he told me about his torturer "Mr. Frederick," who would force prisoners to do lewd sexual actions, punch them in their faces and continually terrorize them. The liberating invaders held nothing sacred. Mr. Frederick made Abdullah stand nearly naked on a flimsy box with wires attached to him, saying he would be electrocuted if he fell off. Abdullah later told me he would sob violently afterwards and had difficulty sleeping due to all he had seen. How it tore me apart to know that Abdullah had been in Abu Ghraib prison, his body often raging with fever.

Abdullah's best friend Ahmet was forced to play with himself in front of the fellow inmates. Sadly, upon his release, Ahmet went home and immediately committed suicide. Nothing undermined the allies' claim that they were helping bring democracy to the country more than the scandal at Abu Ghraib.

I went with some members of the Christian Peacekeeping Team (CPT) who believed in using non-violent methods to solve conflict. They lived and worked amongst the Iraqi people and were warmly received for their sincere effort. Together we went to beseech the American authorities to try and get Abdullah released from prison, only to be met with silence and indifference. We were so concerned about him and his condition. Over 100 prisoners had already died. Our pain was immense. We had lost our families, our homes, our oil, our sons, and now we were losing our dignity through the systematic abuse of Iraqi prisoners.

My cousin Ibrahim ended up working with the Christian Peacemakers (CPT). They were so different than the American occupiers. They did not carry weapons for their personal safety but trusted in the same God that we believed in for protection. Ibrahim later helped form the Muslim Peacekeeping Team who would practice methods of peace to try and diffuse the tensions both between the occupiers and the population, as well as between the various factions of Iraq that were now starting to war against each other.

We could see from working with the Christian peacekeepers that the heart of man was the same the world over. It was governments who divided peoples in their quest for either land, power or resources. Yet, the common people sincerely wanted to live in peace and in a safe world for themselves and for their children.

Later, at university, I would meet many American soldiers and be asked to translate for them because of my knowledge of the English language. I quickly learned that there were two kinds of enemy soldiers. Many soldiers believed they were bringing freedom and democracy; others could see they were doing more harm than good.

When Tom Fox and his friends from the CPT were kidnapped by an insurgent group in late 2005, Ibrahim and his friends were instrumental in gathering the signatures of dozens of prominent Muslim leaders to demand the release of the Christian peacekeepers. It led to Muslim leaders and scholars from all over the world to plead with the hostage takers to let the Christian peace activists free.

The Christian and Muslim Peacekeeping Teams gave hope to people caught in the cycle of violence that there is another way of operating in this world. Meeting people like this kindled hope in me as well. Seeing how Ibrahim changed into such an active peace advocate planted a seed in my heart that would bloom into fruition in the years to come.

Shockingly, after the release of the Christian Peacekeeping Team and the death of Tom Fox in captivity, CTP in a public statement unconditionally forgave their captors.

Our occupiers made a grave error in late May 2003. Paul Bremer, the American head of the Coalition Provisional Authority that ran Iraq after it was occupied by the United States, abolished the ministries and institutions that formed the backbone of Saddam Hussein's power structure along with disbanding Iraq's 500,000-member military and intelligence services. Members of Saddam Hussein's Baath Party were banned from holding government jobs. Disbanding the military, along with the security service, made Iraq an easy prey to its domestic militias and even accessible for terror groups like Al-Qaeda and later ISIS who would in the years to come further terrorize our land and wreak more destruction and death throughout the country.

Many truly welcomed America initially. A large portion of the population of Iraq wanted change. But to outlaw the Baath party was too much. Baathism represented the dreams of many Arabs for a great Pan-Arab nation based on socialism and equality for all. The Arab Baath, or Renaissance Party, was founded by Christians and Muslims together with hopes of unifying the Arab world under the banner of a just socialism free from foreign rule.

Many warned the Americans that this was a bad move, but the American administration thought that they could just throw out the entire old order, and hopefully a new democratic nation would somehow emerge. How foolish they were. It was a decision that would cost the Americans whatever good they had hoped to accomplish in Iraq.

Abdullah was finally released, but one thought continued to race through his mind: How to get revenge on those who humiliated and showed such disrespect to him and his friends. He wanted to help liberate Iraq from the hand of the occupiers. He joined an Al-Qaeda affiliate, not because of their view of theology, but because they had the best weapons and were the most organized in resisting the occupation.

I pleaded with him to stay at home and to help the family. He would reply that the best way to help the family is to liberate Iraq, and that freeing our homeland from all occupiers was the only long term solution.

I reminded Abdullah how our Grandpa had taught us that

the pen is more powerful than the sword. My words fell on deaf ears. Abdullah had made up his mind. He had become convinced that violence would be the only way to resist the foreigners occupying our land. I told Abdullah he was sounding like our invaders who killed to bring us freedom. Why must we kill to find our freedom?

I adored Abdullah. He was my hero, especially after the death of Mohammed. And now I felt like I was losing another brother.

Ya Allah, bring us peace! I longed for the days when Grandpa used to teach us kids the 99 names of Allah. My favorite name for Allah was Al-Wadud, which means the source of all love and affection, all kindness. Grandpa would say we need to fill all our hearts with the love of Al-Wadud and ask Him to remove from us greed and love for the material things of this world. Al-Wadud is an intense, constant affection that is manifested in our action and conduct. He told the children of Rawa that love must be lived in all areas of your life, in deeds, not in word only.

I saw no reason for hope at this time in my life, but I believed the solution had to be in this beautiful name of God, Al-Wadud, and that it would require an incredible amount of love to turn this world around.

8

Anbar University

What Are You Doing Here?

After a student finishes high school in Iraq, most of their interests and thoughts about the future begin with the dream to enter university and go through that wonderful learning experience. Higher education is greatly valued in Iraq.

 I entered Anbar University in late summer 2003. I had a relative, Rami, who was a professor there. He was in a difficult position. There was a suspicious undercurrent of events making it a dangerous job to be a professor in Iraq—many of them in Baghdad and Basra had been killed or disappeared. As a result, tens of thousands of Iraqi academics chose to work abroad, but Rami felt he was safe in Anbar and decided to stay to try to preserve the future of the Iraqi people.

Rana came with me to Ramadi to make sure I was well fed

and so she could have a break from Baghdad. It was a dream of my mother's for me to graduate from university and I wanted to fulfill that dream. My cousin had recently moved to England to get his master's in medicine and I wanted to be like him and study abroad as well one day.

Each day before I left for school, Rana would say a prayer for my safety. We had not heard from Abdullah. He was still in the armed resistance operating in other parts of Iraq. It was like I was all that was left of her family, and though she had become accustomed to tragedy, she was fearful of losing me, too.

I chose to study English Literature with a minor in Computer Science. Anbar University was where I hoped to fulfill many of my aspirations. Unfortunately, my dreams at Anbar University were soon to be shattered. By the end of 2003, the university was forcibly converted to a military base for the U.S. Army.

A university campus is considered a sacred place in most of the world—a place to study, conduct research, and work towards fulfilling one's life's ambitions. It should be a time of learning, discussion, debate; free from violence, conflict, strife. You can imagine the shock the students felt when the rector announced that the U.S. Army would be using sections of the university as a base of operations.

The distance from my off-campus house to the university was 6 kilometers, about four miles. On normal days, it took me 15 minutes to get to campus, but now the streets were full of military checkpoints. I had to get up very early because now it took me almost two hours to reach the university; and with the continual movement of tanks and military vehicles stirring up the dusty roads, the beautiful green foliage of Ramadi was now covered by yellow dirt.

The bitterness of my early morning travels to school led to even greater frustration upon arrival at the university gate. It felt like I was entering a military headquarters—and I was. All students, male and female, were subject to inspection at the entrance. It was difficult, especially for the female students being inspected. Like most of the other students, I felt angry; angry to see our girls going through these embarrassing checks which are not normal in our culture; angry to feel like our sacred halls of higher learning were being desecrated. It prompted us to protest and demand the exit of the American forces from the university campus. Unfortunately, our attempts were unsuccessful and the protests were met with a harsh response by the occupying forces and the arrest of many students.

The only vehicles allowed on campus were heavily-armed military vehicles. Even the rector of the university was subject to inspection and had to enter the university grounds without a car. If we had to attend a lecture at the College of Computers, which is only 800 meters from the College of Arts, it took a long time to go from one building to another. There were two checkpoints between these two buildings.

Can you imagine the questioning I received from the American soldiers at the checkpoint? They had the audacity to ask me, "What are you doing here?" I would always politely reply that, "This is my country and my school, where I am enrolled as a student. What are you doing here?" My calm answers often made my interrogators furious.

Because I spoke English, I did get to know and understand some of the American soldiers. They believed, as they had been told, that they had come to Iraq not to conquer, but to set an oppressed people free. In the early days, they told us their number one priority was to endeavor not to interfere with the general population. Sad to say, their actions proved otherwise.

As time went on, I could see that some of the soldiers began to see that they had been ill-advised, and their actions were counterproductive to what they were sent to do in the first place. I talked with many of these soldiers, and began to pity the simple soldiers occupying our land. I saw them as "duped."

At the end of my first year at Anbar University, on the 28th of June 2004, the U.S. handed over power to an interim government. Ivad Allawi was sworn in as the Prime Minister. Allawi was corrupt. He was put into power to uphold the status quo. His appointment would lead to further unrest and contribute to the ethnic tensions that were simmering.

With the war over, America should have moved into their "peacekeeping" duties. Yet, they resorted to violence to put down protests against the U.S. presence in Iraq, continually firing their weapons into crowds of demonstrators. At the university, boys often shook their shoes at the soldiers (an insult in Iraq), pelted them with stones, and yelled in English, "Down, USA!"

During my four years there things went from bad to worse. On November 19, 2005, a group of U.S. Marines killed 24 unarmed Iraqi civilians in nearby Haditha. The soldiers were going crazier and crazier the longer the war went on. And yet, these soldiers who murdered 24 innocent Iraqis received noticeably light prison sentences. The message was clear; our lives were of no value.

Other soldiers on night missions between towns in the Anbar province, bringing supplies from one base to the other, were ordered to shoot and kill anything that moved. How many innocent Iraqis died due to the over paranoid western occupiers? Most of the American soldiers just didn't get it. They didn't understand how these Iraqis whom they came to "liberate" were choosing to fight against them.

It seems that American ethics are based upon a stark belief in their own righteousness, and the iniquity of the enemy. I think that many Americans were influenced by the myth of American Moral Superiority, causing them to be blinded to their own failings and shortcomings. The United States has accomplished great things, but there's a flip side to that greatness—great power came at great price.

Nearby Fallujah was also a living hell, and the uprisings there were brutally and inhumanely suppressed. Fallujah was the scene of the worst US ground war since 1968. Years after the battles in Fallujah, medical research teams discovered an increase in infant mortality, cancer, and birth defects among children born there. It was later discovered that enriched-uranium exposure from munitions used in the war was a primary or related cause of the birth defects and cancer.

The American media has power to frame events and narratives, and both the media and the military effectively demonize "the enemy." In the battlefield the American soldiers did not see Iraqis as equals, but as inferiors. It was comparable to the cavalry officers fighting the Native Americans in early US history. The outlook was the creed of manifest destiny: "We are right, and this land is our land no matter who lived here before."

I was fascinated by the stories of the Native Americans, and now it seemed to me that just as the early Americans decimated one tribe after another, the story was being repeated in Iraq. The tribes of the desert were being destroyed one by one.

Sadly, at the beginning of my third year of studies, in September 2005, my mentor and relative Professor Rami was gunned down on the way home from work. By the end of 2006 nearly 500 academics had been killed. Was there an organized plan to erase the future of the Iraqi people? It seemed like it. Under the Geneva Convention, the occupying power is supposed to protect the civilians of the occupied country, but much more money was spent protecting the oil fields than the people.

I was being called upon with growing frequency to translate for American soldiers to question the prisoners. Things were getting unbelievably bad in the Anbar province. American Major John Costello called Ramadi the most dangerous place in the world.

We were hurting, but I could see that many of the American soldiers were also hurting. I knew one of them who was involved in the Haditha massacre. He told me how several of his fellow soldiers had been taking enhancement drugs to keep them alert and that contributed to them being overly aggressive. Some soldiers came to my house secretly at night while on patrol to have a break from the stress of night duty. I was being called on to serve as a translator for the military on different occasions, so these men knew me and trusted me.

When these soldiers came into our house seeking rest, as was our custom we served them tea and snacks. Such is the way of our culture. We ended up having long talks, sometimes for hours. I learned from some of these men that quite a few Americans had an inherent distrust in their government due to events such as the Vietnam War, Watergate, etc. I learned once again that our hearts are so similar and that we are both victims of forces and powers outside of our control.

One of my favorite authors, Aleksandr Solzhenitsyn, wrote that "the line separating good and evil passes not through states, nor between classes, nor between political parties either—but right through every human heart . . . even within hearts overwhelmed by evil, one small bridgehead of good is retained. And even in the best of all hearts, there remains . . . an uprooted small corner of evil."

I made friends with a young Mexican man who joined the army to obtain his U.S. citizenship. I thoroughly enjoyed learning some basic Spanish with him and teaching him Arabic. I could see from talking to him that he had many regrets. Sadly, he died one month later from a roadside bomb.

One of the soldiers I'd met committed suicide. My heart broke. We believe that, "If anyone slays a person, it would be as if he slew the whole people, and if anyone saved a life, it would be as if he saved the life of the whole people."[6]

Life is precious to us. The death of one person is the death of a universe. We have been living in the valley of the shadow of death for years now, so we grasp and appreciate life and every moment so much more.

It wasn't until many years later, reading a New York Times article, that I realized that suicide was even deadlier than combat for the American forces, killing over twenty soldiers a day. In just a six-year period (2013–2019) over 45,000 veterans and active duty service members had killed themselves. More soldiers and vets were dying every year due to suicide than from combat in Afghanistan and Iraq.

Studies were being done in America trying to figure out why so many soldiers were committing suicide after returning to civilian life. We knew the reason why. True, they missed the camaraderie they'd had with their buddies in their unit and had difficulty adjusting to civilian life but, the fact is, some of them had killed innocents. How could they live with themselves? Some of them realized that the purpose of the war was not as pure as they'd originally been led to believe. Many were traumatized by the violence they had witnessed and committed. And certainly, the outcome of the war was not what they had expected. How can you live with yourself when you're carrying so much mental and spiritual baggage?

Rana helped me keep my sanity during those tumultuous days at university. More than once, I was put in an

---

6 The Quran. Surah Al Ma'idah 5:32 (abbreviated).

American prison when a roadside bomb went off in our neighborhood. All the young men would be gathered and held for questioning. The temptation to give up my studies and join Abdullah in the resistance was hard to resist. The Americans told me my brother was a leading terrorist. My reply would be to tell them my story, share with them about Abdullah's life and to ask them what they would do if they were born in his shoes? They could not answer me. What could they say?

I graduated in May 2007 at the time of the American surge in Iraq. My graduation from Ramadi should have been a happy time, yet in 2007 things got worse when George Bush and his generals called for a "surge" to rid our province of those resisting the occupation. I knew Abdullah was out there somewhere, fighting. Any joy of my graduation was extinguished by the bloodletting of the time. What was the purpose of all this war? Why did America come here in the first place? Was it truly just for oil?

So many questions lingered in my mind.

9

The Insurgency

Cousin Mustafa's Death

After the 2003 invasion of Iraq and the overthrow of Saddam Hussein, the war didn't end as quickly as it was supposed to. Instead, the Allied Coalition of the United States, Great Britain, Australia, Spain, Poland, and others ended up remaining in Iraq for many years.

The insurgency[7] against these Western forces began shortly after the initial 2003 invasion— the year I started university. It primarily targeted the Allied Coalition troops who were seen as "occupiers" and eventually the Iraqi security forces who collaborated with the Coalition, too.

After Baghdad fell to the Americans, the tribes of the

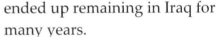

[7] Photo Credit: Author: الإسلام بدر, November 7, 2006 (cropped). https://commons.wikimedia.org/wiki/File:Iraqi_insurgents_with_guns,_2006.jpg

Anbar Province where Rawa and Ramadi are located became stronger because of the political vacuum. They attempted to provide direction and security for the people.

Due to the unfulfilled promises of the Western military occupiers, the Allied Coalition, and the heavy-handed approach taken by the occupiers in the summer of 2003, events spiraled out of control into a full-blown insurgency against the American-led, multinational forces occupying our country. The insurgents were composed of a diverse mix of militias, foreign fighters, and former soldiers opposing the occupation of Iraq by foreign powers.

Many of us had hoped that the American occupation of Iraq would lead to some type of normalcy after two decades of constant war. My fellow students and I had high hopes that things would settle down, and we would be able to enjoy our university years and complete our studies. My roommate would often say "Give me the money that has been spent in fighting over Iraq's oil and I could clothe, feed, and educate every student in Iraq and maybe in all of the Middle East. I could build a schoolhouse in every village and every Arab child would have an opportunity to read and write. I could turn every military base into a sports center for the youth of Iraq."

Sad to say, our hopes for normalcy were shattered! The Geneva Convention states that the occupying powers must protect the civilians in the areas they occupy, but it seemed as if the Americans and the British were only intent on providing security for the oil fields and very little for the people who needed it most. Mercenary armies, with soldiers from all over the world, vigilantly guarded the oil fields at great expense. In our cities and neighborhoods, gangs and militias were being formed to protect their own interests. It was both a frustrating and frightening time.

By September of 2004, the insurgents against the occupation controlled key parts of central Iraq. Abdullah became a leader in the insurgency, leading brazen attacks against the Americans both in Anbar and in Baghdad itself, despite Rana's and my hopes that he'd seek other methods to bring about change. This caused me a great deal of personal grief. However, at the same time, I could understand Abdullah's pain and sorrow.

Abdullah encouraged me to join him in the resistance, but how could I leave Rana to fend for herself? I believed that there had to be another way to achieve peace in Iraq. In my short life, I had already seen the insanity of war take my father, my mother, my elder brother, and two of my sisters. I did not want to see more death. The call for revenge was so loud among the insurgents that the voices for peaceful solutions were often not heard.

The rhetoric of nationalist firebrands like Abdullah and his friends about why the U.S. had invaded Iraq played directly into the hands of organizations like Al-Qaeda and the Shia militias. Al-Qaeda, Shi'a extremists, and other groups exploited the chaos that resulted from the American occupation and their puppet government. These radical elements attempted to hijack the local insurgency for their own purposes. Al-Qaeda's campaign in Anbar went from assistance to intimidation, to murder in the most horrific ways with the sole purpose of driving the people of Anbar to adopt their extremist form of Islam. Abdullah continued fighting against the American occupation but cut all ties to Al-Qaeda. He was heartbroken to see the homegrown Iraqi uprising to regain control of our own country hijacked by these forces with ulterior motives.

This eventually led to a horrible situation where we were being killed both by American soldiers and by Al-Qaeda. Nearly 2,000 civilians were dying each month due to the violence connected to the insurrection and sectarian strife. Iraq was no longer a country but was ruled by different gangs vying for territory and power.

Our province, which was the epicenter of the insurgency, had thousands more American soldiers sent into our towns. I had made friends among the American soldiers who I was called to translate for, and I could see that many of them were like me. They also didn't understand what was going on and why. Yet we were prisoners of events engineered by greater powers that seemed to be out of control. Many of the Marines I knew complained when their tour of duty was extended. They missed their families. I also missed my family, but they were no longer present on this earth.

War is uglier than hell. It only destroys. The war was taking its toll on the human psyche. A well-liked first sergeant I knew shot himself in front of his troops. American soldiers were bordering on mutiny in some areas. They were confused about their mission in Iraq and longed to return to their homes and families, away from the endless wars in Iraq and Afghanistan.

The surge that was instituted by George Bush in early 2007 to provide security to Iraq turned out to be one of the deadliest years we had ever experienced—each year seeming to bring more pain and death.

— ✦ —

The summer of 2007 saw the death of our cousin Mustafa, the well-known local musician. Mustafa took it as his mission to use his golden voice and musical abilities for the benefit of the Iraqi people in their time of suffering. He wanted his voice to spread joy and hope to the Iraqis in their dark hour.

In June, he performed at a wedding of some distant relatives. The wedding party was held out in the beautiful open desert and was coming to a close when all hell broke loose from above. Guests had been firing guns into the air in a sign of celebration before the American helicopter attack blitzed the party killing more than 40 people, including many children and our beloved Mustafa.

That was one of the first of a long list of wedding parties the American military would bomb over the coming years, in both Iraq and Afghanistan. The Western troops were paranoid. They had no understanding of our culture, our tight family bonds, and unfortunately, had adopted a policy of "shoot first and ask questions later."

Rana and I and our extended family were heartbroken over losing Mustafa. Grandpa led the prayers and afterward lovingly reminded us that no blessing would come if we remained in this state of sadness. Allah has ordered that in pressing on in duty, continuing to care for the needs of the many widows, orphans, and those less fortunate than ourselves, that we shall find the truest, richest comfort for ourselves. Light will come again, and through it all we will grow stronger. The load which should have crushed us lifted our souls closer to God. This is the paradox of our lives.

Despite the horrendous errors of the Allied forces in Iraq, the Iraqis ended up siding with the Americans to defeat the outside radical elements coming into Iraq. Dr. Abdul Hamid Al Rawi, from the College of Political Science at the University of Baghdad, told the Americans plainly, "The sheiks have the power to declare that there will be no more attacks on the Americans. If the U.S. works with the tribes in the right way, they might succeed. The tribes could provide security and protection for local directorates, hospitals, schools, and factories. If the U.S. is serious about wanting good relations with the Iraqi people, then it must have good relations with the sheiks."

The Americans listened to Abdul Hamid's advice and the advice of many other sheiks in cooperating together against Al-Qaeda. Al-Qaeda's agenda had become too much for the average Anbari to bear. An agreement was made that U.S. troops had to leave most Iraqi cities and give power back to the sheiks after Al-Qaeda was defeated. The surge initiated by Bush and later with the cooperation of the sheiks of Anbar eventually brought a measure of safety—at a great price. Many American soldiers, rebels, and civilians alike had lost their lives.

Nearly two years after the surge began, on September 1, 2008, U.S. troops returned control of Anbar Province to Iraqi forces. The common man on the street once again felt a small measure of security. The occupation was coming to an end, and at last we would be free to rule ourselves.

It was hard for me to process the events that I had lived through. So many died in vain over the past years. The war began under a false assumption about Iraq's WMD program. The intelligence assessments of Iraq's weapons program before the war had been almost entirely incorrect.

U.S. National Security Adviser Condoleezza Rice admitted that the United States had been mistaken about Saddam Hussein's possession of weapons of mass destruction—the original pretext for the war. When I now lay on my bed in the silent moments, I often wonder, "What reasons could justify all this waste and death?" All that we suffered over the past years, a conflict that consumed hundreds of thousands of lives and billions of dollars, with a massive ongoing cost to the Iraqi people, was for a lie based on misinformation.

On August 31, 2010, Obama declared the end to the seven-year combat mission in Iraq. Little did we realize that less than four years later he would be sending troops back to Iraq—this time to fight ISIS.

10

India

Building a Family

When I returned to Baghdad at the end of my four years at university in Ramadi, another massacre occurred at Nisour Square in central Baghdad. Employees of Blackwater Security Consulting, a private military company contracted by the U.S. government to provide security services in Iraq, shot at Iraqi civilians while escorting a U.S. Embassy convoy. They killed seventeen people and injured twenty.

These killings understandably outraged the Iraqis. In December 2008, the U.S. charged the five Blackwater guards with fourteen counts of manslaughter, then later pardoned them, causing anger and dismay throughout the world. This again made Iraqis feel like their lives were not valued by the U.S.

After finishing university, I left Baghdad and worked for several years as an English teacher in Rawa. There were more tragedies where innocent people died at the hands of paranoid or over-drugged soldiers who thought anything that moved may be a potential enemy. My fellow teacher and childhood friend was killed by American snipers for going outside during a curfew to fix the electrical box. It is unimaginable how many people died for no reason. This man became just another statistic, though in reality, he was someone else's whole universe. He was the world to his beloved family and children.

Our teachers took a monthly collection to help support his widowed wife and children.

At this time, I was suffering psychologically and my relatives were concerned about me. Fortunately, I met my wife to be at this time. She was from the same tribe as I was, and we married early in the summer of 2008. Love healed many of the pains in my heart. We kept our wedding small; no guns were to be fired into the air lest we too become the victims of an airstrike mistaking us for insurgents.

In Spring 2009, we had our first child, a baby boy, whom we named Mohammed after my older brother. It was a miracle to feel the change that came in me. Love and marriage brought healing to my soul that cannot be expressed in words. A new child born into the world is a gift of hope. The belief that maybe, somehow, someway we can make a better world for this child began to take root in my heart. Even if we cannot reach our dreams, maybe if we tell them to our children they will build a better world. Life was starting to look better.

I obtained a partial scholarship to get a master's degree in India so my wife and I and little Mohammed left for India in August of 2009. While living there, we had our second son, Basir. I was happier at that time than I had ever imagined possible.

While the people of India were aware of a war in distant Iraq, most Indians had their own struggles to worry about. It was extraordinarily healing to be in a country where the war drums were not pounding continually, and you could sleep at night without worry about terror or bombs.

I completed my Master's in English Literature. I loved reading the literary greats of the English-speaking world and found joy and beauty in the writings of many.

As I got to know India better I came face to face with man's injustice to man there as well. I made friends with several men from the downtrodden Dalit, the untouchable outcasts in Hindu society. They have suffered for centuries due to the caste system. I broke convention by visiting them in their humble dwellings and having tea with them as well as inviting them to my home for an Iraqi dinner. Twice I was threatened by Hindu nationalists for the kindness I had shown to the "Undesirables."

I reflected on what I had been reading at the time, "Man's Search for Meaning" by Victor Frankl. "[T]here are two races of men in this world, but only these two—the 'race' of the decent man and the 'race' of the indecent man. Both are found everywhere; they penetrate into all groups of society. No group consists entirely of decent or indecent people." How true this is.

I witnessed the truth of Frankl's statement played out in the lives of the American soldiers who occupied Iraq, experiencing startling moments of kindness from a tough, rough-looking soldier who would sneak Abdullah and other prisoners snacks when no one was aware. This was in sharp contrast to prison wardens who would beat prisoners at the slightest opportunity if they were in a bad mood or to avenge the death of a fellow soldier. Truly, human kindness and human cruelty can be found in all groups. The longer I lived, the more I saw that people are pretty much the same the world over and the longings of humanity for peace and the desire for love and acceptance are universal.

Back at school, I became friends with some people who had come from the Democratic Republic of the Congo. Their people, too, had suffered immensely in the early 1900's during the Belgian occupation of the Congo when slave workers would have a hand cut off if they were not working fast enough. Even to this day some of the great powers of the world still fight for the Congo's natural wealth.

It sounded so much like Iraq. I found a strange comfort in knowing we were not the only ones who suffered such things. These stories fed my desire to find answers to the illness of greed and oppression. Was it so simple that power can corrupt a person and once people find great wealth they constantly want more?

I had heard about Mother Theresa who had lived and worked for years with the poorest of the poor in Calcutta, India, caring for, helping and aiding the lowliest of the low. Written on her wall in her humble room were the words:

> *People are often unreasonable, irrational, and self-centered.*
> *Forgive them anyway.*

> *If you are kind, people may accuse you of ulterior motives.*
> *Be kind anyway.*

*If you are successful, you will win some unfaithful friends
and some genuine enemies. Succeed anyway.*

*If you are honest and sincere people may deceive you. Be
honest and sincere anyway.*

*What you spend years creating, others could destroy
overnight. Create anyway.*

*If you find serenity and happiness, some may be jealous. Be
happy anyway.*

*The good you do today will often be forgotten. Do good
anyway.*

*Give the best you have . . . and it will never be enough. Give
your best anyway.*

*In the final analysis, it's between you and God. It was never
between you and them anyway.*

I was struck by beauty of these words—so close, so similar
to the teachings of Islam.

I met many students from Libya in India as well. They, too,
had heart-breaking stories. America and its allies once
again overthrew a Middle Eastern dictator hoping that
somehow, magically, democracy and freedom would
spring up after months of bombing and the complete
destruction of the country's infrastructure.

Libya, like Iraq, ended up in chaos. Obama was applauded
for his honesty in admitting that he made an error in
Libya, but it was far too little, far too late. What did Obama
do to repentantly feed the orphans and assist the widows
he had helped to create, to rebuild their nation, or make it

possible for women to work and become an active part in their society again? Obama's feeling sorry for his errors in Libya cannot be enough. True compassion does something about it. At least, Obama could have built orphanages for the children he orphaned. Libya is another nation which has been sent back to the Stone Age for reasons of political and financial gain by a foreign power.

Women, once so active in Libyan society, are now being sold as slaves on the open market. Women professors were being killed and beaten by the Islamist extremists that temporarily took power after the American intervention. How many more Linda's and Mariam's died? How many younger men became embittered like Abdullah?

My fellow students and I would philosophize and debate over copious amounts of Indian chai about the world of today, God and religion, rich and poor, free and bound seeking for solutions and answers to the wars ravaging our planet.

We loved sharing the jewels we garnered from our studies with each other. One of my favorite was penned by the late James Hilton in his classic novel "Lost Horizon."

> Look at the world today. Is there anything more pitiful? What madness there is. What blindness. What unintelligent leadership. A furiously racing mass of bewildered humanity, strengthening, not in wisdom,

but in vulgar passions, crashing headlong into each other, motivated by greed and propelled into brutality. The time must come when evil will destroy itself.

No words more perfectly described the global plight of 2011 than these—and yet they had been written almost eighty years before. Let's hope when "evil finally destroys itself" that it doesn't destroy the whole world with it!

Our little study group of students that started so informally—finding great enjoyment in one another's company—cultivated the habit of regularly meeting for chai and conversation. Sometimes we'd talk politics; sometimes we'd criticize one another's writings or ideas; other days we'd drift into theology or the state of the nation; always full of good natured banter peppered with joking, puns and hearty fellowship.

Our study group just kept growing. Eventually there were ten members of our little discussion group, always energetically critiquing and refining our thoughts and ideas. Offering each other constructive feedback occupied the better part of our meetings. Nothing could be simpler— a small group of sincere students, meeting most weeks, sitting on a shabby grey couches and old bamboo chairs, drinking, reading, and talking. But as we met extraordinary things began to happen. We forged strong personal connections that have lasted over the years even after the paths of our lives parted.

Our little study group reminded me of something I read describing C. S. Lewis' little discussion group, the Inklings: "Is any pleasure on earth as great as a circle of friends by a good fire?" In our idealism, we felt maybe one day we could make a world where the poor would be fed, clothed, housed, paid a fair wage for their work, and allowed to experience freedom, peace, health, and happiness.

As I was one of the few Muslims in this group, I had to explain to them the true meaning of Jihad[8] or Holy War. True Holy War is not a war of hate and bitterness, killing and slaughter, revenge and vindictiveness. It is not a war for the bodies and possessions and lands and pride of man, which usually only result in more suffering, more hunger, more slavery, bitterness, vengeance, fighting, privation, destruction, poverty and death.

The true Jihad is a war to free men from the evils of the spirit and mind and in the heart of man, which cause them to be unkind, selfish, and cruel to each other—man's inhumanity to man. True Jihad frees us from our greed. How little this is understood.

I longed for peace in Iraq and for peace in the world. One of my favorite poets, the poet Longfellow wrote,

> If we could read the secret history of our enemies, we would find in each person's life sorrow and suffering enough to disarm all hostility.

Somehow, we need to get to know our enemies, reach out to them, and try to understand their struggles. Perhaps small gestures of kindness on an individual level could make a change in the world. Most of our little study group had pretty much given up on changing the world from the top down. We were concluding that change had to begin in one's own heart, then to organically spread to those we know and meet, and from them on to others to affect

---

[8] See "Appendix 3: Chapter Documentation" for Chapter 10.

change in our towns, cities, and eventually the entire nation.

My time in India brought further healing to the many years of suffering and sorrow that I experienced. Little did I know that this time of healing was for a purpose, to strengthen me for what I would face in the near future.

I soon received my master's degree and after enjoying a beautiful two-month holiday in India my little family of four returned to Iraq. That was the summer of 2013. I was determined to turn the sorrow of my past into a beautiful future. I knew it would be a struggle, but I felt better prepared now.

On our return to Iraq, we had a short stopover in the UAE. While at the airport restaurant waiting for the connecting flight home, an American soldier at a nearby table asked if I was from Iraq. When I told him "yes," he profusely apologized for what the USA had done to our country. He was utterly sincere and honest. The world is changing and his sincere apology meant a lot to me. Of course, it could never bring my family back, but I was happy people were starting to realize the truth about what had happened in Iraq.

Upon arrival in Iraq, I moved to Ramadi where my grandfather had settled and Rana was living. Shortly thereafter, a local mosque in Ramadi asked if I would be willing to bring aid to the internally displaced persons in Syria. The chaos from Iraq had spilled over our common border, and Syria had erupted into a civil war in March 2011. It became another Iraq at lightning speed.

It was a great joy to bring aid to Syria. Mom used to say

that if you carry sorrow, the best way to heal your sadness is to help someone else with theirs.

I was on the road to healing!

11

Rise of ISIS

The Valley of the Shadow of Death

Besides taking frequent aid trips to Syria, I started searching for a job at Anbar University. A few months after my return, the drums of war began to beat again, and fighting returned to the city of Ramadi, this time between the Iraqi Army and Daesh.[9] Shells began falling near our house and the majority of our neighbors left the city. We, too, decided to leave Ramadi to go back to Rawa, the town of my birth.

ISIS was turning Iraq once again into a blood-soaked killing field, and Rawa was not spared from the dirty tide due to the sudden withdrawal of the Iraqi Army from the city. Three ISIS command vehicles entered Rawa and took over the town.

ISIS killed Christians, Yazidis, Shias, Sunni Muslims— literally anyone who did not agree with them. They committed genocide and ethnic cleansing on an

---

[9] DAESH is a derogatory term for the terror group ISIS. Muslims call ISIS Daesh to separate them from the true Islamic faith.

unprecedented scale. Some of their favorite methods of execution were beheadings, crucifixions and lining up men in a row and shooting them point-blank. In later years, hundreds of mass graves with thousands of bodies would be discovered in the areas ISIS had ruled, most of it in Anbar Province, where Rawa and Ramadi are located.

In June 2014, ISIS took the historic city of Mosul, to the shock of the world. Mosul, ancient Nineveh, is the second-largest city in Iraq. Our extended family met to discuss the situation, and it was decided that a group of my cousins and their wives, along with my family, should go to Turkey in search of refuge. I had been in Syria, bringing aid to the internally displaced Syrians over the past years, so it was decided that I would lead the team there.

The tribes of Rawa and the Anbar Province did not want to live under the Islamic State. At the same time, Turkey was receiving more refugees than any country in the world after opening its doors to the millions fleeing the violence in Syria. We all felt it would be good if some of the family could move to a safer place. Turkey was not suffering the wars that were ravaging the Middle East. Hell had come to our town before, and what was coming portended to be even worse, so some of us had to go.

Shiite militias had blocked the roads so we could not travel overland to Baghdad and then fly to Turkey, which would have been the safest, quickest way to go. We could not go north through ISIS-controlled Mosul. ISIS was offering amnesty to families who would turn over their sons to the Islamic State to fight, and we didn't want that.

The only clear road was the Syrian border road to the west, so we decided to travel overland to Turkey on this highway. This meant we were in for a long, arduous journey. At dawn on September 10, 2014, we departed Rawa heading towards the Syrian border.

"Ya Allah, ehdina al-Sirāt al-Mustaqīm" was my prayer on the morning of our departure as we entered ISIS-held territory. This phrase, from the Al-Fatiha prayer,[10] has such a deep meaning, both in this life and for the life hereafter. "God, please lead me down the straight and narrow path, though it be an uphill path of difficulty, it is the path that leads to Paradise." It was painfully obvious that the world was on a broad path leading to destruction, but there was safety for the moment in Turkey.

My second prayer was a prayer that Grandpa taught me from the Zabur (Psalms), one of the four Holy Books of Islam. "Though I walk through the valley of the shadow of death, I will fear no evil: for Allah is with me."[11] I would meditate on that every time when crossing the many dangerous ISIS checkpoints.

I was not in the best of moods as I left. ISIS had risen out of the chaos that America and its coalition had left. I was now leaving my grandfather, my uncles, my cousins, and my sister Rana because of it. My heart was heavy, but I had to go to protect my wife, my children, and those traveling with us.

Grandfather could sense my distress, and in his wisdom he

---

[10] The Fatiha prayer is the first chapter of the Quran. Fatiha means the opening. Its importance to Muslims is similar to the importance of the Lord's Prayer to Christians or the Shema to those of the Jewish faith.

[11] The Bible. Psalm 23:4. The Psalms are one of the Holy Books of Islam. They are called "Zabur" in Arabic.

reminded me to look to the Quran, quoting from the Surat at-Tawbah[12] the phrase, "Do not worry. Allah is certainly with us, so Allah sent down His Serenity on the Prophet (PBUH)[13]." Meditating on these ayets (verses) provided tranquility to my troubled mind. Surely Allah is with those who shun evil and do good deeds.

We knew we could die as we traveled through Syria. But we were no strangers to death. Our family, like most in Iraq, had family members or close relatives who had died during the past decades of fighting. We found comfort in our faith. Muslims believe life is God's gift, and we believe that death is predetermined by God, and the exact time of our death is known to God.

We traveled in a van and a car, fourteen of us in total. We knew that there would be many obstacles and numerous ISIS checkpoints. We were treated badly at every checkpoint. They would question us as to why we would want to leave the land of the Islamic State. We said we had several medical patients and needed to go to Turkey for treatment.

Our first stop was Deir Ezzor, the largest city in eastern Syria. At the center of Syria's oil production, Deir Ezzor was a rich city and the ancient site of one of the earliest Christian monasteries. Like Iraq, Deir Ezzor was a mosaic

---

[12] Surat at-Tawbah is a chapter in the Quran. The Quran has 114 Surats or Surahs, depending on how you translate the Arabic word. Surahs / Surats are the equivalent of chapters in English.

[13] The acronym PBUH is used by followers of the Islamic faith to mean "Peace Be Upon Him" when writing or speaking about the holy figures of Islam. Muslims use this to show respect to one of God's prophets when mentioning his name.

of cultures. It was once home to a bustling community of Syrian Orthodox, Capuchin, Syrian Catholic, and Armenian Christians.

Much of Deir Ezzor was captured by groups rebelling against Assad's Syrian regime in 2012, and indiscriminate regime artillery and airstrikes, using old and imprecise weaponry, had wreaked havoc throughout the city. Then, on July 14, 2014, ISIS succeeded in wresting control of most of Deir Ezzor away from both the regime and the opposition. ISIS then systematically eradicated all forms of worship it deemed un-Islamic. While we were there, ISIS demolished a famous Armenian Christian Church in central Deir Ezzor.

We stayed with a distant relative, Ahmet, whose family had moved to Syria nearly a century ago. Rawiyen had moved into Syria as well, and Ahmet's great grandfather settled here years earlier. Ahmet had suffered a lot and had been thrown into prison on false charges. After being tortured and later proven innocent, the regime let him go. He was one of the few fortunate ones to leave the Syrian prisons alive. He never sought vengeance against his false accusers, realizing that vengeance would only lead to more hate and violence.

Later, in 2016, Ahmet left Deir Ezzor to escape from the American bombing of the city in the war against ISIS. In 2018, his entire family—father, mother, and all of his sisters and brothers—would die in a Russian strike on his family's multi-story house.

After leaving Deir Ezzor, we came to an ISIS checkpoint, and an ISIS soldier asked to search our mobile devices. Thankfully, we had no problem with that. Then they insisted on searching the bags of all our women. This is a shame for a man to empty and search the bags of the women. I refused, and a quarrel erupted between us, and he shot bullets in the air. A higher officer came out and after questioning us allowed us to go.

We crossed 28 ISIS checkpoints before reaching Tal Rifaat, the final crossing, before entering the territory held by the Free Syrian Army that borders Turkey. This was the final, most difficult ISIS checkpoint. The interrogation lasted 45 minutes. The ISIS border guards asked us religious questions, looking for a weakness in our knowledge of the Quran. If the guard would find one, he could say we were infidels and we could be killed. Thankfully, I know the Quran well. One interrogator got upset and threatened me when I showed him an error in his understanding of the Quran. It was a mistake that could have jeopardized our little company, but we were finally allowed to pass after what seemed like an eternity.

In the areas controlled by the Syrian Free Army, the treatment was good. As soon as they knew that we were from Iraq they made it easier for us, but even here, there were hidden dangers such as snipers belonging to the Syrian regime forces that terrorized travelers, forcing us to change course and use a very bumpy country road that eventually reached Turkey.

Being very tired, we finally reached the Syrian-Turkish border. We entered Turkey at night and went to a hotel in the border area before traveling the next day to a city in southern Turkey where we were to settle.

We had left Iraq just before Ramadi was almost totally destroyed. The campus in Ramadi, where I had studied and had so many friends, was attacked by ISIS gunmen in late 2014, and secured by them in 2015. An estimated 16,000 students and academics were killed or displaced. The university looked as though it had been hit by an earthquake with around one-third of buildings destroyed and the laboratories looted. By the summer of 2015, ISIS would control 90% of Anbar Province.

It was almost impossible for the weak and fragmented government of Iraq to get rid of ISIS by itself. The government had to look to help to defeat ISIS from an international coalition again led by the U.S.—the perpetrators of the whole mess to begin with.

Sad to say, shortly after we arrived in Turkey, Rana called us saying she had received a phone call from a stranger using Abdullah's phone. The voice on the other end of the phone told her, "The person who owns this phone is dead." Then the phone clicked off.

Once again my world came tumbling down about me. Everything I held precious seems to disappear. My heart pains to think that Abdullah was one of the thousands buried in one of the ISIS mass graves later discovered in Anbar Province and surrounding Mosul. The irony of the whole matter is that Abdullah, who once fought against America and was considered a terrorist, died fighting against ISIS, one of the enemies of America.

Rana and I had discussed several times whether Abdullah had actually been a "terrorist" for fighting against the coalition of nations occupying Iraq. There was no doubt in our mind, Abdullah was not a "terrorist" as some accused him of being.

We knew Abdullah's nature growing up and how as a child he would not harm a thing. We saw him change, though, due to the injustices he lived through—the series of tragedies inflicted upon us by foreign powers seeking to control Iraq's oil.

So many Iraqis lost their livelihoods and their homes, but the western nations controlled our resources. If we tried to retaliate, they would call us "terrorists." It's like being robbed by a gunman. You scream and holler because you were robbed. You then punch the thief because he stole from you. But then the robber screams and yells, "He hit me! He hit me! This guy's a terrorist! It isn't fair!" . . . And the onlooking world listens to the thief, but not to the victim. The victim state, not the thieving state, becomes labelled as the terrorist state. How is that fair?

It justifies aggressor countries to carry on wars and murder hundreds of thousands of people based upon lies. How unfairly the world looks at things. "There are none so blind as those that will not see!"[14] They don't want to see it.

The occupying powers were additionally guilty of state terrorism by not ensuring the safety and protection of the civilians they were supposedly liberating. The Western nations were attempting to impose their ideologies of democracy upon us, but the means they used did not justify the end, an end which they never achieved.

Rana and I easily concluded that there is not much justice in the world. It is obvious. Justice in this world is all too often on the side of those who have the biggest guns and

---

[14] The Injil (Gospel), Matthew 13:13.

the best technology. Sad to say, "Might makes right."

Man at his best, which is truly his worst, is in the field of war. In war, mankind uses his greatest creative genius and inventive power to design new ways of destruction. How sad and what a waste of the human mind to spend time producing weapons of war and murder!

Plato wrote, "The curse of me and my nation is that we always think things can be bettered by immediate action of some sort, any sort, rather than no sort." Sometimes it is wise to wait. There are seasons when to sit still demands greater strength than taking action and resorting to violence.

The Western nations should have known that when you fight fire with fire you only get more fire. The more we pick up the sword the more we die by it. There must be another way. Violence is a failure of imagination and a gross lack of patience. May God give us peace.

How different our world might have been if the foreign powers had waited and not intervened. Change would have come to Iraq naturally, and we are assured that it would have been better than the change these outside countries tried to bring swiftly through war, occupation, and violence. Because they have no other way to follow, they turn to their weapons of war to solve problems.

We were left to suffer all alone, totally alone.

12

My New Life

Beauty for Ashes, Joy for Sorrow

Arriving in Turkey, I had no problem finding a job at one of the many Syrian schools in southern Turkey. At the time, Turkey had well over three million Syrian refugees.

At first I taught at one of the U.N. schools for Syrians. When those closed, I volunteered with different charities, usually as a translator or delivering aid. This gave me the opportunity to work full-time with Syrian refugees. Even though I did not have a stable income, I felt this was my duty to my God.

Sadly, the war in nearby Syria was becoming deadlier with each passing day. The Syrian Civil War, unfortunately, is a war that is next to impossible to stop. It is being fought as a global proxy war between the USA, Russia, and China. On a regional level, Iran and Saudi Arabia are vying for power in Syria. Locally, different religious and ethnic groups are warring against each other. How could you get all these factions to sit at one table to talk about peace?

In late 2016, during the terrible siege of Aleppo, I traveled to the Syrian border to bring aid to the families who had managed to leave Syria through the safety corridor. On one occasion I was the guide for a volunteer from the UK, Shazad, who was bringing aid to the border region along with Talal, another Syrian volunteer.

 We weren't prepared for what we were about to see on the Turkish-Syrian border. We entered a little hut about a football field's distance from the Syrian border. It had nothing but torn plastic in the window frames. The tiny entrance room was filled with ten little children and a single father and two mothers looking after them. The children were from three different families, eking out a living together on the edges of this border town.[15]

The father and two surviving mothers were struggling to take care of this group of children. Some of children had lost their mother to a sniper's bullet while they were passing through eastern Aleppo's humanitarian corridor to leave the war zone.

It was almost too much for our Syrian volunteer, Talal, to be with us on the border, seeing his beloved country so close, where his parents, sister, and little brothers still resided. He had not seen them in four years, and the emotional struggle was intense for him. He desperately

---

[15] A child who loses their mother or their father, but not necessarily both, is considered "an orphan" in Syria. Some of these children had lost both!

wanted to cross the border to see his loved ones but could not. He risked being killed or forced into one of the many factional armies. The difficulty of Talal's emotional battles found some temporary relief in the refugee children we found. He hugged the orphans and told us, "When I hug them, I see my little brothers who I miss so much."

Shazad, Talal, and I went to town, found, and hired a laborer to put real windows into this little home. We also bought some good quality mattresses to replace the thin, worn mats they were sleeping on. And Shazad gave them a large enough financial gift to get them through the next few months.

There are many other stories to tell, such as that of a widowed mother living in a run-down, one-room house without electricity with six children, all of whom were ill. Our little Turkish charity adopted this family, providing them with a better house and furniture.

It was a time of profound contrast: the deep sadness when a widow shares her story, versus the sweet abiding joy you find when a child's face lights up in laughter after receiving a simple gift.

One time we came across a young man burnt beyond recognition, who only wanted to drink tea with us just to be able to sit with someone who was not afraid of his looks. How can you heal a heart that is so broken? We were wishing we could do so much more, while asking why there had to be so much death and suffering. Yet we also rejoiced, rejoiced in the resilience of so many who had lived so close to death and yet were so full of life—but their lives will be scarred for a long time.

Widows broke down in tears when we handed them some cash and brought them a few weeks of provision to help their desperate situation. They were so thankful to taste a little bit of heaven after so much hell. Hope was realized— there are people in the world who do care.

Refugees value the moment. There is no past, it has been destroyed. The future is uncertain and cloudy. All they have is now. When having tea with these refugees, the conversation was vibrant, all were present. They are beautiful people, thankful to be alive. We often forget the beauty of "now" in our impersonal, fast-paced modern world.

Syria itself took in many refugees in previous decades. They welcomed the Palestinians after the 1948 and 1967 Middle Eastern wars. During the Lebanese Civil War, they took Lebanese refugees into their homes. They housed well over a million Iraqi refugees during the Gulf Wars. And now, in their hour of need, they are considered outcasts to much of the world. Yet somehow a beauty shines through. Beauty born in the midst of the ashes of defeat.

There's a certain joy and contentment not known by most, but which those who have experienced such deep heartache and sorrow often find. I marvel at times how refugees in the midst of extreme hardships are able to serve others with joy.

Elisabeth Kubler-Ross wrote,

> The most beautiful people we have known are those who have known defeat, known suffering, known struggle, known loss, and have found their way out of the depths. These people have an appreciation, a

sensitivity, and an understanding of life that fills them with compassion, gentleness and a deep loving concern. Beautiful people do not just happen.

Only from such depths of sorrow can spring forth such joy, beauty and appreciation.

Friendships develop at warp speed when you are in a war zone. At the end of Shazad's visit, after spending three full days bringing aid to orphans and widows, Talal broke down and wept. It is difficult to see a 24-year-old man cry. Through his sobbing, a pure melodious heart cry rang out from the absolute depths of his being in a high-pitched tone crying, "I want my mother." There was absolute silence in the room.

The sweetest of songs come from such pain.

At that moment I think we all longed to be a child again, safe on our mother's gentle breast; we longed for the purity and simplicity of childhood and to be far, far from the nightmare we were now witnessing. We longed for comfort, comfort for Talal and for the refugees we visited. There wasn't a dry eye in the room, and in our crying out to the unknown, to the distant past, to a mother, to God, inexplicably, we found peace in our hearts.

How I wish that all of those who make weapons and who support war could come to the Turkish-Syrian border and see and talk with the many orphans, the tens of thousands of limbless young men and women, a mother with no legs struggling to watch her toddler, the widowed mothers and fathers living in storefronts, lying on a ragged mats on the floor, trying to raise their children or the orphaned children of their friends or relatives; to witness the children with burns . . . it hurts to look at them, it hurts to write more. Those who visit the refugees on the border cry out for all wars to end—no more war!

Now, as I tell others about that border trip, my tears flow naturally when I recall the beautiful children living in such poverty and loss, yet somehow still maintaining their childhood. My heart weeps.

We relived our Aleppo experiences all over again from September 2019 to March 2020 when Russia and the Syrian regime bombed the Idlib Province, destroying eighty medical facilities and displacing over 900,000 other Syrians.

The U.N. Humanitarian Chief, Mark Lowcock, told the Security Council that shelling by Syrian and Russian forces in Idlib Province risked creating the worst humanitarian disaster of the 21st century. He asked the Security Council, "Are you again going to shrug your shoulders . . . or are you going to listen to the children of Idlib, and do something about it?"

While the Security Council has failed time and time again, I see that it is the kindness of aid workers, volunteers, donors and sponsors who are making a quiet difference.

J. R. R. Tolkien said it best through Gandalf in "The Lord of the Rings:"

> Saruman believes that it is the only great power that can hold evil in check. But that is not what I have found. I have found that it is the small things, everyday deeds of ordinary folk, that keeps the darkness at bay.

During this time period, we organized regular shipments of wood, blankets, tents and other items to the needy in Idlib living in informal tent settlements. It was a drop in the bucket compared to the huge need of the many displaced people who had lost their homes, but we also knew our gifts would go a long way and meant a great deal to the recipients. Our trips inside Syria are another story in itself, one that if it were told would fill page upon page with heartbreak and sorrow.

There has been a sharp rise in the number of cancer cases amongst children in Iraq and Syria. Another by-product of endless wars? I see and experience it daily in the three children's medical homes I work with. The homes are funded by a small Turkish charity. I find meaning and a deep, abiding joy helping these children through these tough times. Not all the children survive, and for those who don't I try to make their exit from this world as quiet and comfortable as possible.

I also find surcease to the pain in my life by helping these others who are hurting. I have discovered that a genuinely happy life is a life lived for others. You can discover such fulfillment in laying down your life for another, even for strangers. Actually, I have come to realize that there are few real strangers, most are only friends that I have not yet met.

I believe that in the greed of our world today, many have

lost the joy of giving. There is the belief that our happiness comes from material possessions, when happiness and greatness lie not in what we have but in what we give. An honest look at the world today will show us that having many things brings only temporary, fleeting satisfaction. Who do you know that is really happy because of what he or she has? Yet, I do know people who have nothing and have a jubilance in life as if they possess everything.

The Quran says that "Allah is the most Loving, Al Wadud." Wadud is different from "al-Hub," the Arabic word for love. Al-Wadud is derived from the word "al-Wud," which means an expression of love through the act of giving. As we endeavor to take on the attribute of Al-Wadud, the laying down of our lives to serve one another in love and kindness, we find the Salam, the Peace, that all believers seek.[16]

---

[16] The Quran. Surat al Buruj 85:14.

13

Conclusion

The Power of Love vs. the Love of Power

Since the age of nineteen, when the USA and a coalition of Western powers invaded our country for a second time, I have had nearly two decades to reflect upon the events that have shaped my life. I have studied history in depth. Can we learn from history, or are we doomed to repeat our past mistakes? How true is the statement from historian Arnold Toynbee who said, "The only thing we learn from history is that man never learns from history."

These sordid chapters of history continue to repeat themselves. "History:" I read it and I weep. How true is the saying of the wise prophet Suleyman, who said, "He who increases knowledge, increases sorrow".[17] Someone else said that "history never repeats itself, but it often rhymes," each couplet more disruptive than the one before. The more I have studied the clearer it has become to me that the world is once again heading towards difficult days of massive proportions unless we learn from the errors of the past.

---

[17] The Book of Ecclesiastes 1:18.

America, China, and Russia today are similar to a great empire that was in power millennia ago in our timeless land of Mesopotamia, that of ancient Assyria. Despite positive contributions to mankind in the use of iron and engineering skills, Assyrians are also remembered for their cruelty. They earned the nickname the "Lords of Torture."

Nebuchadnezzar of Babylon was also quite barbaric in his collection of foreign kings that he conquered. I would venture to say that even though man has now learned to sanitize his crimes, the atrocities of modern nations are equally as appalling.

War has progressed to the point that fighting is now clean. Drones fly at altitudes miles high over hostile towns, and a drone pilot on the other side of the world, in an air-conditioned military office, fires a missile at an enemy target.

Power is a plague to mankind. Both Jesus and Mohammed told us to seek Allah and His Kingdom first, not power. We don't handle power well. Instead of using power to serve, once we have power it corrupts us, and we want others to serve us. Power is given so that we can serve mankind, not have mankind serve us.

The great prophets of Christianity and Islam taught us the proper use of power, but the words of the prophets are no longer heard in the world today. Mohammed, the Messenger of Allah (PBUH), said, "If anyone relieves a believer from one of the hardships of life, Allah will relieve him of one of the hardships of the Day of Resurrection. If you make it easy for one who is indebted to you, Allah will make it easy for you in this worldly life and the hereafter."[18]

Jesus the Messiah (PBUH) succinctly expressed the correct use of power in the Gospels. He told his followers to be servants of all. "It shall not be so among you. But whoever would be great among you must be your servant . . ."[19] Sad to say, these words are too often looked upon as poetry, not as a way to fashion one's life.

Long ago, I concluded that western nations are just as guilty of some of the crimes that Saddam had committed. Rather, the western invaders have cloaked their motives for destroying Iraq with a mantle of self-righteous hypocrisy, declaring it a "just war."

We are blind to our own faults. Everyone believes that they are the good guy, so how can we see clearly to cast the speck out of another's eye when we cannot first see the beam blocking our own vision? I was saddened to read that Christian evangelicals were big supporters of the Iraq invasions when their own Messiah taught them to love their enemy. Those in the West condemn violence in the Middle East yet they continually overlook the terrible reign of death unleashed upon the people of this region by their own governments.

To this day, when the question comes up again if Abdullah was a terrorist, I explain that we see him as a victim of great and powerful outside forces that took away everyone that he loved and rained terror upon our land for decades. We see the Western world, blinded by its greed and

---

[18] Hadith 36.

[19] The Gospel (Injil) Matthew 20:26.

endless hunger for our resources, as guilty of forcing our fun-loving brother into a life of hate and revenge.

I think most people in the West would have made the same choices if they had been born in Abdullah's shoes and lived his life instead of theirs. It is so easy to dismiss one's enemies as evil, but if we took the time to listen and understand, we might see how similar we are and in the process, disarm our "perceived" enemy.

It has become too easy to castigate "Islam" as being inherently violent and yet completely disregard the obvious impact of contemporary history. ISIS, which is as Islamic as the KKK is Christian, might simply be a byproduct of America's and Britain's wanton adventurism in and beyond the Middle East. Simply put, the Iraq War was a failure that created the Islamic State, and devastated the entire Middle East.

I am convinced that further violence in the beautiful Middle East will only breed more violence. I still remember my mother telling Abdullah that "those who live by the sword will one day die by the sword" before he went off to join the insurgency. She pleaded with him not to bear weapons. The power politicians of this world would do better to listen to a mother's intuitions. It seems only mothers know that we are all losers in a war: Nobody ever wins a war—everybody's a loser! All the dead and broken bodies, suffering and sadness, sorrow and pain.

War is too often the default policy of nations. Money put into war and weapons of war are wasted, a total absolute loss. When we were students, several times we discussed what would happen if all the world's weapon factories stopped producing weapons and instead we used this money for education, agriculture, the arts, and the advancement of humanity. What a world that would be!

A previous American president, President Eisenhower, having been a leading general in the Second World War, said:

> Every gun that is made, every warship launched, every rocket fired signifies, in the final sense, a theft from those who hunger and are not fed, those who are cold and are not clothed. This world in arms is not spending money alone. It is spending the sweat of its laborers, the genius of its scientists, the hopes of its children.

Insightfully, he went on to state:

> The cost of one modern heavy bomber is this: a modern brick school in more than 30 cities. It is two electric power plants, each serving a town of 60,000 people. It is two fine, fully equipped hospitals.

> We pay for a single fighter plane with a half-million bushels of wheat. We pay for a single destroyer with new homes that could have housed more than 8,000 people.

> This is not a way of life at all, in any true sense. Under the cloud of threatening war, it is humanity hanging from a cross of iron.

Sad to say, Eisenhower's words fell on deaf ears. During the year 2020, an American bomb exploded every nine minutes somewhere around the world. Every death by these weapons means a new orphan, a child without a father, or a widow left struggling to survive. There has to be a better way to solve problems than by war.

I still have a hard time coming to grips with the fact that well over 600,000 innocent Iraqi civilians died due to the fact that several nations falsely concluding that Iraq had weapons of mass destruction or was involved in any way with the 9/11 tragedy. Americans rightly weep for the three thousand who died in the Twin Towers but are insensitive to the sufferings inflicted upon us during their relentless aerial bombings and "shock and awe" campaigns.

Perhaps in their drinking deeply of the intoxicating doctrine of American superiority and exceptionalism and the idea that they have a unique mission to transform the world, they are blinded by their supposed moral superiority.

It is going to take radical steps of forgiveness to reverse the cycle of revenge and destruction still taking place in our lands. Somewhere, somehow, we have to begin, to start, to break down the walls of hate with gestures of love. God has 99 names, but perhaps one of the greatest of these is "al Wadud"—Love. Love and outgoing concern are the only ways forward. They are the antidote to evil.

We have hope of a new world rising from the ruins of the old through the message of peace, love, and the preservation of life and truth by all the simple people of the earth who still believe in love and serving humanity. Then, at last, "nation shall not lift up sword against nation, neither shall they learn war any more"[20] as incised into the

---

[20] The Book of Isaiah 2:4.

wall of the U.N. building in New York.

Until that day of peace comes, I will keep trying to change things from the bottom up. I will continue to teach my dreams to refugee children, and maybe they will one day build a better world from the broken pieces of our dreams.

I will plant an apple tree today, even though the world plans for war tomorrow.

Appendices

From the Author

I met the real Mahmoud four years after the story I told in
Romania in 2014 to the young people and staff at the little
hostel where I stayed after my hiking journey in the
Carpathian Mountains. Though his story is different than
the one I told back then, I used a few parts of his story in
this book. He, too, is a man who has lost so much, but
through it all he has found satisfaction and meaning in life
through serving others.

I have been working with Mahmoud for more than three
years now and our work has gotten national recognition.
The UN visits our medical homes for Syrian refugees
regularly. Thanks to the teams and individuals around the
world who fundraise for this cause, thousands of dollars of
aid have been donated to refugees in the form of food
assistance, scholarships for girls, housing for refugee
children receiving medical treatment while in Turkey and
aid trips to the Syrian border and into Syria.

Working with refugees has provided some wonderful
moments that will be treasured forever. There have been
times of tears, heartbreak and sorrow after hearing their
stories. After my first visit to the Syrian border, I was not
able to talk about what I had witnessed without getting
teary-eyed. I had not realized just how deeply the events I

experienced affected me; so many fatherless children who wanted to show me a photo of their deceased father (after some time I began to think this was the new norm, to be an orphan); photos of little Hiba before her nine operations to restore the right side of her face and her burnt-off ear.

Through it all I felt as if I was being taught by these refugees about life, hope, and joy in the midst of such suffering. I have sat with refugees in the most squalid conditions, on bare cement floors, in little cold tents, trying to keep warm with a cup of tea and huddled around a little wood heater, if they were fortunate enough to have one.

So often when talking with refugees, their conversation would be sprinkled with thanks and Alhamdulillahs for what they have, thanking God during trying times and even thanking God for their difficulties. At times I feel as if I have lived my life in a pampered nursery, complaining if my coffee is not the way I want it. My refugee friends make me more aware of my many blessings. We have a lot to learn from them!

When with some refugees, you feel something tangible, perhaps bordering on holy. The Psalmist David wrote "God is close to the brokenhearted,"[21] and maybe this is what we sense. Those who have lived on the threshold of death, the brokenhearted, often find life more valued and precious. The simplest things often bring them great joy.

The "now" is all many refugees have to enjoy, even if it is only a simple meal shared with a stranger. This is the truth for all of us — that we only have "now", the present

---

[21] Psalm 34:18

moment, but somehow we don't always catch it.

During the initial years of working with refugees, I worked with Talal, himself a Syrian refugee and a university student. He had previously lived a good life in Damascus but had needed to start all over again in Turkey.

Even though our generations, ethnicities, and cultures were thousands of miles and decades apart, Talal and I became close friends while working with refugees. Working on life-and-death situations can bring you together as nothing else can. As we worked one evening on a presentation for a European Union meeting on refugees, we were discussing the latest news from Aleppo, which was under intensive bombardment at that time.

Talal questioned, "Why does God let Syria suffer so much?" At the end of 2010, over 1,300,000 refugees from around the Middle East and asylum-seekers were housed in Syria — over 6% of the country's population at the time. Talal's father also worked assisting Iraqi refugees, and after all the help they gave to others Talal's family is now scattered throughout Europe, the Mideast, and some still in Damascus. Due to the lack of medical aid available in Syria, Talal's youngest brothers have multiple health problems.

On the Syrian border, Talal and I met mothers whose sons died before they ever really lived. We also met limbless sons who wanted to die, wishing they had never lived. Questions like Talal's question about why is there so much suffering are so difficult to answer.

I always feel sad when I hear the song "What Becomes of the Brokenhearted?"

The chorus haunts me. No answer is given:

> What becomes of the brokenhearted,
> Who had love that's now departed?
> I know I've got to find some kind of peace of mind,
> Help me ...

I wonder what happens to all the broken and lonely people in the world. I know we can not help everyone and heal all the wounded hearts but it is such a beautiful thing when people come together from all over the world to reach out to a refugee trying to survive. It makes a big difference to the one they help.

We once rented a home for a year for a widow and her two children who had been living in a garbage depot. We know that a brokenhearted person now has new hope! Once she was able to get into a proper house, her son found a job, and now she can make it on her own and is on the road to healing.

My earnest desire through the publishing of this book is that people will be inspired to reach out to others who are marginalized and to choose peace and dialogue as solutions to conflicts that arise. Anything is better than war and strife or even the torment of not living in harmony with our neighbors. If there is anyone you do not understand, sit down together and relax over a tea or a cup of coffee with them and watch friendships grow and blossom, and you will be richer for it.

Thank you for purchasing this book. All proceeds will be given directly to refugees, to help clothe those who are cold, feed those who are hungry, give drink to those who thirst, and look after those who are sick.

We stand with refugees, those who have been despised and denied of their dignity. We stand with those who are too often considered undesirable and unwanted. Please stand with us!

Shukran! Thank you!

— Jon Rose

Chapter Documentation

Photo story of the overarching time period

The Iraq War | Council on Foreign Relations
https://www.cfr.org/timeline/iraq-war

Chapter 1: Iraq—The Cradle of Civilization

Rawa Hospitality, New Haven Restaurant

Soul Of Iraqi Village Surfaces In Westville
https://www.newhavenindependent.org/index.php/
archives/entry/rawa/

Chapter 2: My Early Years

. . . there is evidence that Kuwait was engaged in slant-drilling of Iraqi oil, under the border. As one oil executive put it, slant-drilling is enough to get you shot in Texas or Oklahoma.

It's Time to Think Straight About Saddam
https://www.nytimes.com/1997/12/23/opinion/IHT-its-time-to-think-straight-about-saddam.html

Iran-Contra Affair

Iran Contra affair
https://en.wikipedia.org/wiki/Iran%E2%80%93Contra_affair

Russian Supply of Weapons to Iraq

Russia to become Iraq's second-biggest arms supplier
https://www.bbc.com/news/world-europe-19881858

Chapter 3: Invasion of Kuwait

Gulf War Documents: Meeting between Saddam Hussein and US Ambassador to Iraq April Glaspie
https://www.globalresearch.ca/gulf-war-documents-meeting-between-saddam-hussein-and-ambassador-to-iraq-april-glaspie/31145

We have no opinion on your Arab-Arab conflicts, such as your dispute with Kuwait. Secretary (of State James) Baker has directed me to emphasize the instruction, first given to Iraq in the 1960's, that the Kuwait issue is not associated with America.

U.S. Ambassador Glaspie

Sex Slaves in Kuwait

Women from Sierra Leone 'sold like slaves' into domestic work in Kuwait | Employment
https://www.theguardian.com/global-development/2015/apr/02/women-sierra-leone-sold-like-slaves-domestic-work-kuwait

Filipino workers treated like slaves in Kuwait
https://www.manilatimes.net/2018/02/22/news/top-stories/filipino-workers-treated-like-slaves-kuwait-officials/381833/

Human trafficking in Kuwait
https://en.wikipedia.org/wiki/Human_trafficking_in_Kuwait

Kuwait and Saudi Arabia PR Blitz for Gulf War I

U.S. Congressman Jimmy Hayes of Louisiana—a conservative Democrat who supported the Gulf War—later estimated that the government of Kuwait funded as many as 20 PR, law and lobby firms in its campaign to mobilize U.S. opinion and force against Hussein. Participating firms included the Rendon Group, which received a retainer of $100,000 per month for media work, and Neill and Co., which received $50,000 per month for lobbying Congress. Sam Zakhem, a former U.S. ambassador to the oil-rich gulf state of Bahrain, funneled $7.7 million in advertising and lobbying dollars through two front groups, the "Coalition for Americans at Risk" and the "Freedom Task Force."

Deception on Capitol Hill
https://www.nytimes.com/1992/01/15/opinion/deception-on-capitol-hill.html

Nayirah's Lying Testimony

How PR Sold the War in the Persian Gulf
https://www.prwatch.org/books/tsigfy10.html

Nayirah testimony
https://en.wikipedia.org/wiki/Nayirah_testimony

The Nayirah testimony was a false testimony given before the United States Congressional Human Rights Caucus on October 10, 1990, by a 15-year-old girl who provided only her first name, Nayirah. The testimony was widely publicized and was cited numerous times by United States senators and President George H. W. Bush in their rationale to back Kuwait in the Gulf War. In 1992, it was revealed that Nayirah's last name was al-Ṣabaḥ and that she was the daughter of Saud Al-Sabah, the Kuwaiti ambassador to the United States. Furthermore, it was revealed that her testimony was organized as part of the Citizens for a Free Kuwait public relations campaign, which was run by the American public relations firm Hill and Knowlton for the Kuwaiti government.

Wikipedia, December 2020

Amid Deprivation, Emir's Palace Is Gleaming

Kuwait: Efforts to rebuild the plush quarters are defended, even as city struggles to restore basic services.

> https://www.latimes.com/archives/la-xpm-1991-03-19-mn-491-story.html

Before all the public utilities were restored, the Emir of Kuwait had his palace refitted with golden toilet seats. In this war-ravaged city with no running water or electricity and growing desperation and despair, the U.S. Army Corps of Engineers supervised the sumptuous restoration of the Emir's Palace.

"Democracy, Not Dictatorship"—The Washington Post

Saudi Arabia Beheadings

Saudi Arabia Set a New Record by Beheading Over 180 People in 2019 https://www.businessinsider.com/saudi-arabia-sets-record-beheading-over-180-people-in-2019-2020-4

Saudi Arabia carrying out 'unprecedented wave' of executions
https://www.bbc.com/news/world-middle-east-34982154

Capital Punishment in Saudi Arabia

Rare footage of public beheadings in Saudi Arabia
https://www.middleeasteye.net/fr/news/rare-footage-shows-public-beheadings-saudi-arabia-318277846

- Beheading with a sword is the most common form of execution.

- Executions are often carried out in public.

- Crimes that carry the death penalty include murder, adultery, treason, gay sex, drug offences, sorcery and witchcraft, and apostasy.

- Human rights activists say those accused often do not receive fair trials.

- The families of prisoners facing the death penalty are not always informed in advance of executions.

Chapter 4: The First Gulf War

Gulf War I

6 Things to Know About Operation Desert Storm
https://www.military.com/history/operation-desert-storm-6-things-know

Though many details remain classified, interviews with those involved in the targeting disclose three main contrasts with the administration's earlier portrayal of a campaign aimed solely at Iraq's armed forces and their lines of supply and command. Some targets, especially late in the war, were bombed primarily to create postwar leverage over Iraq, not to influence the course of the conflict itself. Planners now say their intent was to destroy or damage valuable facilities that Baghdad could not repair without foreign assistance.

The worst civilian suffering, senior officers say, has resulted not from bombs that went astray but from precision-guided weapons that hit exactly where they were aimed — at electrical plants, oil refineries and transportation networks. Each of these targets was acknowledged during the war, but all the purposes and consequences of their destruction were not divulged.

The bombardment may have been precise . . . but the results have been felt throughout Iraqi society, and the bombing, ultimately, may have done as much to harm civilians as soldiers.

Some critics, including a Harvard public health team and the environmental group Greenpeace, have questioned the morality of the bombing by pointing to its ripple effects on noncombatants.

The Harvard team, for example, reported last month that the lack of electrical power, fuel and key transportation links in Iraq now has led to acute malnutrition and "epidemic" levels of cholera and typhoid. In an estimate not substantively disputed by the Pentagon, the team projected that "at least 170,000 children under five years of age will die in the coming year from the delayed effects" of the bombing.

A campaign to incapacitate an entire society . . . may be inappropriate in the context of a short war against a small nation in which the populace is not free to alter its leadership.

Gulf War Air Campaign
https://en.wikipedia.org/wiki/GulfWar_air_campaign#:~:text=The%20air%20campaign%20of%20the,destroying%20military%20and%20civilian%20infrastructure

The Highway of Death

The War Photo No One Would Publish
https://www.theatlantic.com/international/archive/2014/08/the-war-photo-no-one-would-publish/375762/

Thirty years Ago. The 1991 Gulf War: The Massacre of Withdrawing Soldiers on "The Highway of Death"
https://www.globalresearch.ca/remember-the-1991-gulf-war-the-massacre-of-withdrawing-soldiers-on-the-highway-of-death/767

Joyce Chediac, a Lebanese American journalist wrote: "It has often been said that the images of the still controversial slaughter on the highway to Basra were so graphic that they shocked the first president George Bush into immediately calling off the ground war after only 100 hours after viewing the charred and dismembered bodies of tens of thousands of Iraqi soldiers, who were withdrawing from Kuwait on February 26th and 27th 1991 in compliance with UN resolutions.

U.S. planes trapped the long convoys by disabling vehicles in the front, and at the rear, and then pounded the resulting traffic jams for hours. "It was like shooting fish in a barrel," said one U.S. pilot. On the sixty miles of coastal highway, Iraqi military units sit in gruesome repose, scorched skeletons of vehicles and men alike, black and awful under the sun, says the Los Angeles Times of March 11, 1991. No survivors are known or likely. The cabs of trucks were bombed so much that they were pushed into the ground, and it's impossible to see if they contain drivers or not. Windshields were melted away, and huge tanks were reduced to shrapnel.

The massacre of withdrawing Iraqi soldiers violates the Geneva Conventions of 1949, Common Article III, which outlaws the killing of soldiers who are out of combat. To attack the soldiers returning home under these circumstances is a war crime. Iraqi forces were leaving Kuwait voluntarily, and that the U.S. pilots were bombing them mercilessly."

On the inland highway to Basra is mile after mile of

burned, smashed, shattered vehicles of every description—tanks, armored cars, trucks, autos, fire trucks . . ." The inhumane destruction littered the highway from Kuwait City to Basra.

Time Magazine. March 18, 1991

Amiriyah Shelter Bombing

Amiriyah shelter bombing
https://en.wikipedia.org/wiki/Amiriyah_shelter_bo mbing

Amiriyah bombing 30 years on: 'No one remembers' the victims
https://www.aljazeera.com/features/2021/2/13/amiri yah-bombing-30-years-on-no-one-remembers-the-victims

Remembering Amiriyah
https://sojo.net/articles/remembering-amiriyah

A Precedent: The Korean War

In the North's capital Pyongyang, only around 50,000 people out of a prewar population of 500,000 remained in 1953, the year the war fizzled out.

When all the cities, towns and industrial sites were destroyed, U.S. warplanes bombed dams, reservoirs and rice fields, flooding the countryside and destroying the nation's food supply. In one of the Shediac most infamous atrocities of the war, between 163 and 400 men, women and children were gunned down at No Gun Ri in South Korea over three days in July 1950. Retreating South Korean and U.S. troops also blew up bridges teeming with refugees, and during their retreat from the North; they burned villages and towns in a "scorched earth" policy to deny the advancing enemy quarters and supplies.

General Curtis "Bombs Away" LeMay—who commanded firebombing raids on Japanese cities that killed more civilians than the nuclear bombings of Hiroshima and Nagasaki—served as strategic air commander during the Korean War.

He would later acknowledge that "over a period of three years or so, we killed off 20% of the population" of North Korea. That's nearly 1.9 million men, women and children. In comparison, the Nazis had murdered 17% of Poland's pre-World War II population just a few years earlier.

Americans have forgotten what we did to North Korea
https://www.vox.com/2015/8/3/9089913/north-korea-us-war-crime

US destruction of North Korea must not be forgotten
https://asiatimes.com/2020/06/us-destruction-of-north-korea-must-not-be-forgotten/

Chapter 5: The Devastation of Economic Sanctions

Iraq: War's Legacy of Cancer
https://www.aljazeera.com/features/2013/3/15/iraq-wars-legacy-of-cancer

A 1995 Lancet study sponsored by the United Nations Food and Agricultural Organization concluded that 576,000 children under the age of five perished because of the economic sanctions policy, while a "conservative" estimate put the death toll for the same age group at 350,000.

Dennis Halliday resigned from the organization (UN) in protest after spending a little over a year as the UN Humanitarian Coordinator in Iraq. He said the sanctions constituted genocide. His successor, Hans von Sponeck, also a career UN employee, lasted just two years before stepping down in protest; Jutta Burghardt, then head of the World Food Program, did the same.

Were Sanctions Worth the Price?—In These Times

The reason Iraq's economy was "run down" and its infrastructure decimated has more than a little to do with a massive American bombing campaign during the first Gulf War, followed by 13 years of the most comprehensive sanctions in the history of the United Nations. Bremer's "surprise" at Iraq's devastation is like a Union general arriving in Atlanta after Sherman and expressing shock that the place had been torched.

Razing the Truth About Sanctions Against Iraq
https://www.gicj.org/positions-opinons/gicj-positions-and-opinions/1188-razing-the-truth-about-sanctions-against-iraq

When Iraq Was Clinton's War
https://www.jacobinmag.com/2016/05/war-iraq-bill-clinton-sanctions-desert-fox/

American Assassination

Swans Commentary: Iraqi Silent Genocide
http://www.swans.com/library/art7/jlind001.html

American Assassination: The Strange Death Of
Senator Paul Wellstone
https://www.amazon.com/American-Assassination-
Strange-Senator-Wellstone/dp/0975276301

U.S. Senator Paul Wellstone who compared sanctions
to genocide, mysteriously dies.

The destruction of the Iraqi people was, after all,
completely planned by the United States. A Pentagon
document dated January 18, 1991 reads, "Iraq depends
on importing specialized equipment and some
chemicals to purify its water supply . . . Failing to
secure supplies will result in a shortage of pure
drinking water for much of the population. This could
lead to increased incidences, if not epidemics, of
disease . . . The entire Iraqi water treatment system
will not collapse precipitously. . . . full degradation of
the water treatment system probably will take at least
another 6 months." The same embargo that banned the
importation of water purifying chlorine a decade ago
still exists to this very day, over ten years after the
time when epidemics of cholera, hepatitis, and
typhoid were predicted to occur.

Iraq Water Treatment Vulnerabilities Memo

The results, needless to say, have been devastating.
Iraq, once the most prosperous country of the entire
Middle East, had become one of the least (March 1999
UN Report). Access to potable water, relative to 1990

levels, is only 50% in urban areas and 33% in rural areas. The overall deterioration in the quality of drinking water has contributed to the rapid spread of infectious disease (World Food Program). And the fact that government drug warehouses and pharmacies have few stocks of medicines and medical supplies due to the sanctions only adds gasoline to an already unquenchable fire.

World Health Organization, February 1997

The Clinton Years

In 1999 alone, the U.S. spent $1 billion dropping bombs in Iraq; in 2000, that number was up to $1.4 billion. Can you imagine how that money could have saved all the suffering children not just in our country but the entire Middle East?

From the end of Operation Desert Fox until the 2003 invasion, the U.S. and UK bombed Iraq at least once a week—all under the guise of enforcing the no-fly zone. We lived in a state of continual insecurity.

Disgusted with the situation, Hans von Sponeck, the UN humanitarian coordinator in Iraq at the time, took it upon himself to compile reports on the airstrikes. In 1999 alone, he documented an average of one bombing every three days, killing a total of 120 people and injuring 442. The West ordered countless air strikes against Iraq because it was unable to cooperate with United Nations (U.N.) weapons inspectors yet many UN inspectors gave a different report that we indeed were complying.

Chapter 6: Gulf War II

Scott Ritter
https://en.wikipedia.org/wiki/Scott_Ritter

The Death of Mom and Linda

Smart bombs aimed at Saddam killed families
https://www.telegraph.co.uk/news/worldnews/mid
dleeast/iraq/1428061/Smart-bombs-aimed-at-
Saddam-killed-families.html

2pm: Saddam is spotted. 2.48pm: pilots get their
orders. 3pm: 60ft crater at target
https://www.theguardian.com/world/2003/apr/09/ir
aq.julianborger

Concentrated Aerial Onslaught

1990-1991: Desert Holocaust
https://williamblum.org/chapters/killing-hope/iraq

Smart Bombs Miss Iraqi Targets
http://news.bbc.co.uk/2/hi/middle_east/1184086.stm

US Quietly Admit They Bombed And Killed
Innocent Family In Iraq
https://newspunch.com/us-bomb-innocent-family-
iraq/

Sand and Dust Storms
https://www.researchgate.net/publication/27604893
0_Sand_and_dust_storm_events_in_Iraq

Sandstorm Clouds Are Gathering for Troops in
Southern Iraq
https://www.nytimes.com/2003/03/23/international/
worldspecial/sandstorm-clouds-are-gathering-for-
troops-in.html

Chapter 7: Torture

The Hooded Man
http://100photos.time.com/photos/sergeant-ivan-frederick-hooded-man

Sergeant Is Sentenced to 8 Years in Abuse Case
https://www.nytimes.com/2004/10/22/world/middleeast/sergeant-is-sentenced-to-8-years-in-abuse-case.html

Who can forget the Abu Ghraib prison?
http://www.albiladdailyeng.com/can-forget-abu-ghraib-prison/

Christian Peacekeeping Team Hostage Crisis

Christian Peacemaker hostage crisis
https://en.wikipedia.org/wiki/Christian_Peacemaker_hostage_crisis

Chapter 8: Anbar University

Most dangerous place on the planet, Ramadi

Marine veterans of deflated by city's fall to ISIS
https://www.scpr.org/news/2015/05/21/51841/marine-veterans-of-ramadi-reflect-on-citys-fall-to/

Death of the Professors

Who Assassinated Iraqi Academics?
https://fpif.org/who_assassinated_iraqi_academics/

U.S. Troops Fire on Iraqi Protesters, Leaving 15 Dead
https://www.nytimes.com/2003/04/29/international/

worldspecial/us-troops-fire-on-iraqi-protesters-leaving-15.html

The Massacres

US marine pleads guilty to Haditha killings
https://youtu.be/-TI0yR68tqI

Ex-Blackwater Guard Nicholas Slatten Sentenced to Life for Nisour Square Massacre
https://original.antiwar.com/Brett_Wilkins/2019/08/15/ex-blackwater-guard-nicholas-slatten-sentenced-to-life-for-nisour-square-massacre/

Fallujah, The Hidden Massacre
https://www.gicj.org/videos-and-medias/757-fallujah-the-hidden-massacre

The Blackwater Shooting
https://www.nytimes.com/video/world/middleeast/1194817114268/the-blackwater-shooting.html

US troops kill 13 Iraqi protesters
https://www.theguardian.com/world/2003/apr/29/iraq.sarahleft

Suicides

Suicide Has Been Deadlier Than Combat for the Military
https://www.nytimes.com/2019/11/01/opinion/military-suicides.html

Why Soldiers Keep Losing to Suicide
https://www.pbs.org/wgbh/frontline/article/why-soldiers-keep-losing-to-suicide/

Sergeant Murders fellow soldier and then Commits
Suicide
https://www.stripes.com/news/us/army-closes-
investigation-into-allegations-of-a-coverup-in-2007-
murder-suicide-in-iraq-1.634431

The Destruction of Ramadi

After ISIS: Inside the Iraqi City Left in Ruins
https://abcnews.go.com/International/isis-inside-
iraqi-city-left-ruins/story?id=39073778

Ramadi Aerial Picture
https://commons.wikimedia.org/w/index.php?curid
=16322641

Chapter 9: The Insurgency

The Insurgents

Al-Anbar Awakening
https://www.hqmc.marines.mil/Portals/61/Docs/Al-
AnbarAwakeningVolII%5B1%5D.pdf

The Surge

Why Did Violence Decline in Iraq in 2007?
https://www.jstor.org/stable/23280403?seq=1

Mutiny

U.S. Soldiers Stage Mutiny, Refuse Orders in Iraq
Fearing They Would Commit Massacre in Revenge
for IED Attack
https://www.democracynow.org/2007/12/21/us_sold
iers_stage_mutiny_refuse_orders

Mustafa's Death

Wedding party massacre
https://www.theguardian.com/world/2004/may/20/iraq.rorymccarthy

U.S. Helicopter Fires on Iraqi Wedding
https://apnews.com/article/47bc1acb7d22b2d8fbc5bf934fe06b37

The US Has Bombed at Least Eight Wedding Parties Since 2001
https://www.thenation.com/article/archive/us-has-bombed-least-eight-wedding-parties-2001/

We were all wrong, says ex-weapons inspector
https://www.theguardian.com/world/2004/jan/29/usa.iraq

The Sheiks

In the Sheiks' Hands
https://www.smh.com.au/world/middle-east/in-the-sheiks-hands-20031110-gdhr2q.html

Tribalism is in our culture; even the urban populations adhere to its customs—hospitality and generosity, honor and honesty. "I think the U.S. was totally unaware of this side of our culture till about a year ago. We tried to tell them, but the problem with the Americans is they think that anyone who talks and walks like them is a good guy and that they can work with them. But if people look different and dress differently, or if their religious or cultural principles are alien to them, they must be a bad guy and so should be avoided.

The average Iraqi doesn't see the Americans reopening a school or a hospital. But they do see their lives being continually disrupted, so they become humiliated and disgruntled. Throw into that the terrorist activity of the remnants of the Saddam regime and the influx of Islamic groups that the Americans have allowed over our borders and you can see that the U.S. is creating a phenomenal number of enemies who, after 35 years of dictatorship, are more than willing to pick up a weapon and vent their frustration on easy targets.

Al-Sharif Ali Bin-al-Husayn

Chapter 10: India

Understanding Jihad

In its most general meaning, jihad refers to the obligation incumbent on all Muslims, individuals, and the community, to follow and realize God's will: to lead a virtuous life and to extend the Islamic community through preaching, education, example, writing, etc. Jihad as struggle pertains to the difficulty and complexity of living a good life: struggling against the evil in oneself—to be virtuous and moral, making a serious effort to do good works and help to reform society.

The two broad meanings of jihad, non-violent and violent, are contrasted in a well-known prophetic tradition. Muslim tradition reports that, when Muhammad returned from battle he told his followers "We return from the lesser jihad to the greater jihad." The greater jihad is the more difficult and more important struggle against one's ego, selfishness, greed, and evil.

> "Jihad: Holy or Unholy War?" John L. Esposito, Professor of Religion and International Affairs and Islamic Studies at Georgetown University and Director of the Center for International Studies.

Chapter 11: The Rise of ISIS

Destabilization of the Middle East, the Rise of ISIS

Enough Already: Syria
https://youtu.be/dK7U5OmGU_A

Iraq crisis: Islamic State accused of ethnic cleansing
https://www.bbc.com/news/world-middle-east-29026491

https://www.dw.com/en/gruesome-evidence-of-ethnic-cleansing-in-iraq/a-17894173

It's time to be real: what happens in Iraq is ethnic cleansing
https://www.worldwatchmonitor.org/2019/07/its-time-to-be-real-what-happens-in-iraq-is-ethnic-cleansing-journalist/

Iraq: More than 200 mass graves with thousands of bodies discovered
https://www.worldwatchmonitor.org/coe/iraq-more-than-200-mass-graves-with-thousands-of-bodies-discovered/

The Body Collectors of Mosul
https://www.bbc.com/news/av/world-middle-east-43965282

Deir Ezzor

The Churches of Deir Ezzor
https://www.atlanticcouncil.org/blogs/syriasource/the-churches-of-deir-ezzor/

Bomb-damaged Syrian church holds first service in 6 years
https://www.worldwatchmonitor.org/coe/bomb-damaged-syrian-church-holds-first-service-6-years/

Rawa set free from ISIS

Iraqi forces recapture final IS-controlled town, Rawa
https://www.bbc.com/news/world-middle-east-42026801

Missing men and unemployment weigh heavily in Iraqi Euphrates River Valley
https://www.trtworld.com/magazine/missing-men-and-unemployment-weigh-heavily-in-iraqi-euphrates-river-valley-22249

Chapter 12: My New Life

Iraq's Generosity

Iraqis Are World's Most Generous to Strangers
https://www.reuters.com/article/us-global-charity-index/iraqis-are-worlds-most-generous-to-strangers-global-survey-idUSKCN12O2RX

Al Wadud

And He is the Oft-Forgiving, Full of Loving-Kindness.
The Quran, Surat Al-Buruj (85:14)

Exploring One of Allah's 99 Names: Al-Wadud
https://www.amaliah.com/post/35625/exploring-
one-of-allahs-swt-99-names-al-wadud

Al-Wadūd: The Most Loving, The Most Affectionate,
The Beloved, The Loving-Kindness

From the root w-d-d which has the following classical
Arabic connotations: to love, to be affectionate, to
long for, to desire, to wish for.

For further Study

Shock and Awe
https://www.youtube.com/watch?v=0yr-LaMhvro

How The US Lost Hearts And Minds In The Iraq
War
https://youtu.be/if7r9dm61b4

Western Iraq | Institute for the Study of War
http://www.understandingwar.org/region/western-
iraq

Iraq is falling apart. We are ruined
https://www.theguardian.com/world/1999/apr/24/d
avidsharrock

Duncan Hunter: Iraq unit 'killed probably hundreds
of civilians'
https://edition.cnn.com/2019/06/01/politics/duncan-
hunter-barstool-interview-killed-
hundreds/index.html

Visiting Iraq on Culture trips

Discover the Unseen Beauty of Iraq With 'Adventure Not War'

https://theculturetrip.com/middle-east/iraq/articles/discover-the-unseen-beauty-of-iraq-with-adventure-not-war/?amp=1

What Becomes of the Brokenhearted?

As I walk this land with broken dreams
I have visions of many things
But happiness is just an illusion
Filled with sadness and confusion
What becomes of the broken-hearted
Who had love that's now departed?
I know I've got to find
Some kind of peace of mind
Maybe . . .

The roots of love grow all around
But for me they come a-tumblin' down
Every day heartaches grow a little stronger
I can't stand this pain much longer
I walk in shadows searching for light
Cold and alone, no comfort in sight
Hoping and praying for someone to care
Always moving and goin' nowhere
What becomes of the broken-hearted
Who had love that's now departed?
I know I've got to find
Some kind of peace of mind
Help me . . .

I'm searching, though I don't succeed
But someone look, there's a growing need

Oh, he is lost, there's no place for beginning
All that's left is an unhappy ending
Now, what becomes of the broken-hearted
Who had love that's now departed?
I know I've got to find
Some kind of peace of mind

I'll be searching everywhere
Just to find someone to care
I'll be looking everyday, I know I'm gonna find a way
Nothing's gonna stop me now
I'll find a way somehow
And I'll be searching everywhere
I know I gotta find a way
I'll be looking . . .

— Jimmy Ruffin[22]

---

[22] Born May 7, 1939, Jimmy Ruffin is an American soul singer, and
elder brother of David Ruffin of The Temptations. He had several hit
records between the 1960s and 1980s, the most successful being "What
Becomes of the Brokenhearted."

Safe Haven for Refugees

All proceeds from *The Story of Mahmoud* book sales will be donated to Safe Haven for Refugees and will go directly to support our four medical homes where refugee children with cancer and their caretakers reside.

Safe Haven is a 501(c)(3) charitable organization. It operates from the USA on a shoestring budget. Our office consists of a computer in a basement; our volunteers are a group of concerned individuals who provide lifelines and support for the most desperate cases of refugee families—especially widows and orphans—in southern Turkey and along the Syrian border.

Safe Haven also provides support for the education of many refugee families' children, and strategically partners with Anything for A Smile, a Turkish registered association that works with the local Red Crescent and other international charities.

To know more about Safe Haven for Refugees visit our website at www.safehaven4refugees.org, and Anything for A Smile at http://www.hsbgi.com/en/home.

About the Author

 John Scott is an educator and one of the founders of Safe Haven for Refugees. He has been living in Turkey for over two decades and has been working with refugees since the Syrian refugee crisis began.

John uses the pen name Jon Rose as it is the name he used to open his social media accounts years back and is the name most of the refugees know him by.

Printed in Great Britain
by Amazon